By

the

Howling

Cyberworld Publishing

www.cyberworldpublishing.com

ISBN 978 0 9808011 1 8

Cyberworld Publishing is an imprint of
Puppy Care Education *publisher*
Jindalee St, Toronto, Asutralia

Other books by Olivia Stowe

Fiddler's Rest

By the Howling

Olivia Stowe

Chapter One

Charlotte looked around as she nosed the Penguin into the ramp and hauled herself unceremoniously—and, she was sure, quite clownishly—up on her belly onto the rough and splintery wooden planks of the pier adjacent to the ramp.

"Feel one with the boat," she muttered to herself as she pulled on the small sailboat, repeating the instruction she'd been given in the crash course on sailing she'd taken back in Annapolis. The problem, however, was that she felt like she was more than her share of that "one" with the small, single-person sailboat—not more than a dinghy, really. She was sure, though, that if she was going to get the hang of this sailing business, it was going to be in a Penguin-class sailboat. She was much too heavy for the lighter Sunfish, and the sleeker and faster Laser was something she knew, with a mind to how difficult it had been for her to move from typewriter to computer, that she couldn't handle no matter how hard she tried. And anything requiring more than one person was utterly out of the question. She was definitely, unequivocally a one-person person now.

1

With a grunt and several groans she struggled up to her knees on the rough surface of the pier. This wasn't easy to do while being careful not to let loose of the line attached to the Penguin, which was bumping gently against the thick wooden poles holding up the pier in the waters of the northward bend of the Choptank River.

On her two feet now and sloughing off the slight vertigo she felt at being on dry land, she looked around into the yards of the neighbors on either side of her to make sure she wasn't putting on a show worthy of admission before she worked to haul the small craft up the ramp and onto the grass and saw, in half dismay, that she wasn't alone after all.

"What are you looking at?" she asked in mock belligerence.

But Sam just sat there and looked at her, his tongue hanging out, and a silly grin on his face.

"This isn't going to be a pretty sight, Sam," Charlotte said. "I suggest you stay well back. In fact, I'd retreat all the way back to Susan's back porch, if I were you."

The Siberian husky just sat there and watched her with baleful eyes. Then he raised his head, eyes planted in the sky, and took a deep breath, preparing to howl.

"And we'll have none of that, young man," Charlotte said sternly. "You'll wake the dead with that howl of yours and the whole neighborhood will come running to watch Charlotte Diamond make a fool of herself yet again."

Sam must have gauged both the tone of Charlotte's voice and her admonition as serious stuff, because he lowered his head again and remained silent.

He also, however, remained planted in the observer's section of the back lawn and seemed to enjoy immensely Charlotte's huffing and puffing efforts to pull the Penguin up onto the grass of her yard.

"They said I'd find sailing out on the river restful and calming," she muttered to no one in particular. "I guess what they meant by that was that it would send me to my final rest—in the grave."

Still, she felt pleased with herself that she had actually gotten the boat out into the river and not only was able to maneuver away from the dock but was able to reach home again. She'd always said she'd rather be sailing; it had been a roving joke in the department—especially after the lads had discovered she'd been on no boat smaller than the Queen Mary. And now that she had the time on her hands—time weighing her down at every corner, actually—she was determined to enjoy sailing if it killed her. Which, the way she felt now as she tried to stand up straight again, it might.

She turned to give Sam's ear a playful tug before she walked up the steep path to the back door of her cottage—knowing that the dog the neighbors, the Wellses, had left behind for their house sitter to take care of while they were gallivanting off on an archeological dig in Turkey, enjoyed this attention and that Susan, the house sitter didn't like or understand dogs well enough to render the service. But Sam was gone.

That was so like the husky Charlotte had become accustomed to the six months since she had retired to the waters of the Chesapeake Bay. The hound was so strong and powerful-looking, almost wolf like, always seeming to be taking a pose, ready to take a leap and yet rarely moving a muscle. And yet, if you turned your eyes aside, it will have taken a silent bounder half way across an open field, looking back at you with laughing "catch me if you can" eyes. It was so much like some scoundrels Charlotte had come into contact with in her professional life that, if Sam were hers, she would have named him Bandit.

As she trudged up the short hill and past the screened porch that jutted out on the back of her clapboard cottage, Charlotte wondered if she'd really have the courage to continue with the sailing routine. It was hardly a routine, of course, as this was only the third time she'd ventured out onto the river. But Charlotte wasn't anything, if not determined. And she was resolved to have fun no matter how painful it was, and she steeled her resolve to go out on the river again on Wednesday, this being a Monday—or maybe on Thursday or Friday. She wondered how many times she'd need to have this fun before the cost of the Penguin was justified.

Charlotte was having a hell of a time settling on just what she wanted to do with herself in retirement. She had agreed to take on the position of mayor of her small Eastern Shore Maryland village, Hopewell on the Choptank, within a few weeks of moving to this idyllic setting—which was one week longer than it had taken her to become totally bored with retirement life. But that lofty position had been no more than becoming a sounding board for gripes by people who hadn't changed their pet peeves and feelings of injustice and outrage in three-quarters of their lifetime. She wasn't in the position for more than a couple of days before it became obvious to her that it was a sucker job that was foisted off on all newcomers to the village.

Not that Hopewell on the Choptank—Hopewell for short, of course—was one of those rural riverine villages lost in time and place, where the locals made fun of and preyed on city slickers moving to a sleepy paradise where time moved slowly and everything was roses and clover. Indeed, almost the whole Eastern Shore was like that. But Hopewell was an enclave, where everyone seemed to be an artsy-fartsy interloper who had done something fabulous in world capitals before retreating here. So the village in its entirety was held at arm's length by the grinning locals, who shook their heads at all of the arts and crafts and expensive simple-life hobbies the folks of Hopewell came up with to pretend that they were having fun. And of course they could never stop trying to achieve, to reach the top of some status heap.

Sailing had been one such fantasy for Charlotte—but it wasn't the only new "meaningful" activity she was trying to master to make up for having become an instant nobody the day she had driven out of Annapolis. And as she approached the kitchen door to her cottage and looked up into her dining room window, she remembered that her sailing had been just to fill in the time before the meeting of her book club—which was to happen within a half hour—in her own parlor.

What jolted her memory about the impending meeting was what she didn't see in her dining room window. In planning for the book club meeting, Charlotte had organized in her mind what she would use to serve refreshments. And the antique Japanese porcelain tea set she had placed on the table in front of the dining room window when she'd moved in leaped to her mind—the set that had belonged to Sydney's mother and that both he and his secretary, immersed as she

5

was in the tacky modern vinyl style, had refused to take when they trotted off and left Charlotte in the dust.

Her former mother-in-law, Gladys, had always said that reading was a waste of anyone's time. She had even tried to haul off all of Charlotte's nineteenth-century novels to a jumble sale that time Charlotte and Sydney had taken the Atlantic cruise on the Queen Mary—the trip that was so confining that it dawned the revelation in Charlotte that there was little about Sydney that she could tolerate any longer, and in Sydney that his secretary was a lot more fun than Charlotte was. Which was neither here nor there, of course, except that Charlotte liked Sydney significantly more than she'd ever liked his mother, and had thought that using Gladys's prized Japanese tea set for her reading club was just too delicious to resist.

Trotting into the dining room from the kitchen had similar results to what Charlotte hadn't seen from the back stoop. The Japanese porcelain tea service still wasn't there. And now, not only did Charlotte have to take a quick sponge bath and find something to wear that didn't make her look like a whale, but she also had to come up with another idea on what to serve the tea in—and she didn't have time to sleuth the mystery of the missing tea pot. Which, if truth be known was the most comfortable activity she could have been engaged in. But she simply didn't have time for that now. She was too busy enjoying her leisure time.

Charlotte wasn't nearly as upset that the tea set wasn't there as she was at the probability that she had moved it someplace else and forgotten to tell herself where it had gone. That was precisely why she had been out sailing that morning, was hosting a book club meeting

6

within minutes, and later in the afternoon was scheduled for a preliminary meeting of the art show judges panel she, as mayor—and certainly not as someone with an eye for art—had agreed to sit on. Before she had retired—forcibly so, by the law of her trade—Charlotte had made the mistake of reading a magazine on retirement. One article had assured her she couldn't afford to retire, even though she had no choice in doing so, while another one that stuck in her mind cheerfully reported that most retirees drifted off into dementia soon after leaving their jobs because they no longer had anything meaningful to occupy their minds with.

Charlotte was terrified, at least under all of that "let's pretend" in her jolly surface dealing with her new life, that her mind would go before her body did. And maybe, just maybe, not remembering what she had done with the tea service was a signal of that happening already.

With a sigh Charlotte forced this gnawing fear out of her mind and headed for her bathroom—searching her mind as she moved on to wondering where she might have put her bath sponge. It didn't help her one bit that she couldn't remember what book they were supposed to be discussing at today's meeting—and, on top of that, was quite certain she hadn't read it anyway.

As it turned out, whatever book they were going to discuss that day was the last thing in anyone's mind.

Chapter Two

Charlotte barely had time to dress, start the tea to boiling, and pull out the packages of cookies that looked deceptively as if they were home baked before she heard the bickering of the Vales on her front walk. Joyce and Todd had been in the village longer than most anyone else. They owned the local quaint B&B up River Street, with a dining room that claimed to serve the best crab cakes on the Eastern Shore—which indeed all restaurants on the Eastern Shore claimed. But at least a famous novelist had declared their crab cakes the best, so that's what the travel magazines grasped upon to highlight in their little vignettes on the amenities of Hopewell on the Choptank. Nowhere is it mentioned, though, that Joyce was the famous novelist's editor at Random House in her earlier life and that he was still so terrified of her that he would have endorsed anything she'd asked him to bless.

For Joyce, living in Hopewell had two attractions. The village had been an artists' enclave that suited her literary interests after a career as a high-powered book editor for a major publishing house, but also this was a returning to her roots affair for Joyce. The B&B had been her childhood home. There was less of a rationale for her husband, Todd, to be here—much less. From the way he blustered around town and had his hat in every organizational ring, it was pretty clear that retirement and retreat hadn't been his idea at all. And, although, a remarkable talent for abstract oil painting had been jerked out of him by the classes at the newly opened arts center, there was no hint that he enjoyed the prospect of spending his declining years in an enclave like this. Whereas Joyce's pursuits had continued to be in the arts, even in semiretirement, Todd had headed up the fraud unit at an international-level cutthroat insurance agency, GML, and cutthroat business maneuvering was deeply engrained in his approach to life, even in sleepy Hopewell.

Charlotte had no idea how—or even why—Joyce had dragged him to the book club meeting. He usually avoided such things like the plague, and the way he was hanging onto her arm and yapping in her ear as they approached the cottage gave Charlotte the impression that he didn't realize where Joyce was headed and just wasn't finished with whatever fight they had started back at the B&B.

They were still arguing when they swept into the cottage. Rachel Sharp, the village doctor, was hard on their heels and immediately began rearranging the furniture in Charlotte's parlor—which she had carefully arranged herself the previous evening so that there was a space for her to bring a dining room chair in for herself at the last minute that would be as far away as possible from the most comfortable wingback chair, where Charlotte knew that Grady Tarbell, a former professor, of inane boredom, would maneuver his voluminous backside. The professor, who still taught something only

9

remotely usable part time at the venerable Washington College in Chestertown up peninsula from the Choptank had been on the make for Charlotte since she had moved to Hopewell, and she had no interest in taking on a Sydney Number Two.

Somehow mousey Jane Cranford had slipped in when nobody noticed—which was so like Jane anyway—and had taken the wingback chair. Grady had brought in a dining room chair and plopped it right next to Charlotte's Boston rocker, which, by the time everyone settled, was the only place left for Charlotte to sit. So, she remained standing and sort of hovered around pretending to be a hostess, when, truth be told, she didn't have the first notion of what hostesses did. The other truth to be known was that Charlotte hadn't sat in the Boston rocker for years, as she was afraid that it just wasn't up to supporting her weight. And when Grady had invited her to sit for the fourth time, she said as much.

"I feel like a whale," she declared, half hoping the image would cool Grady's interest. "I was out on the river today in the Penguin and I felt like a whale in a tea cup there too—and if I sat in that rocker, I think I'd feel like a whale in a teaspoon on land—and I'd be more likely to capsize that than I was the Penguin."

"You were out on the river in a Penguin?" Jane asked, and she said it in such a way that she implied it was a miracle Charlotte hadn't slopped the water from the river up into the streets of Hopewell.

Charlotte turned a gimlet-eyed stare on Jane. It was one thing for Charlotte to talk about her weight; it was quite another thing for Jane to do so. Jane was so thin that the only way to be sure she was in the room was to view her straight on. Not for the first time, Charlotte resolved to run a name check on Jane. The book was that she had been a cabaret singer who had married a New York mobster of some wealth and eventually of several bullet holes and that Jane had retreated here with his money. But that story was very hard to swallow. Charlotte did have to accept, thought, that Jane was an accomplished landscape artist, because Charlotte had seen her paintings in Annapolis galleries before she'd ever seen Jane in the faded, scant flesh.

"Yes, she was, I saw her out there," Todd Vale said. What he didn't say, though, was how good she looked wearing the Penguin.

"Nonsense, Charlotte," Rachel said, "you're not fat; you're just zaftig. And being twice as tall as the rest of us—"

Charlotte tuned out the rest of that statement, although it was nice to have a doctor coming up with an exotic-sounding name for it—and she'd never had a doctor say she wasn't overweight yet. Perhaps she would change from the overpriced GP in Annapolis to Rachel's care.

"Statuesque," Grady chimed in. And if a professor of the arcane could manage a lustful leer, Grady Tarbell was doing it.

Charlotte swung away from that, and her attention dropped immediately into the bickering Joyce and Todd were doing.

". . . and if you hadn't had your eyes on the river," Joyce was saying, "you'd have seen the silver walk off."

"Walk off, nothing," Todd responded. "You've just put it away somewhere and forgot that you did so or where it is. You did the same with that pearl necklace last week, and we still haven't found—"

"I did not misplace it, Todd Vale."

11

"Funny you should mention that," Grady chimed in, talking more to the fireplace than to anyone else in the room—and as easily ignored by all assembled. "I went to look for my stamp collection the other day, and it wasn't where I thought I'd left it. I always keep it right there on the top right corner of my desk in the study, right next to the statue of Newton I found in a dusty hole-in-the-wall antique store near Covent Garden. Of course I've always thought I spent a bit too much for that statue. Very interesting—and rare now—interwar stamps from Germany. I found one just like it in Cape May in the summer of '87 for a lot—"

"I wish," Joyce's voice rose over Grady's and she puffed her ample bosom up. "I'd never let you buy that retirement magazine that—"

"You are missing some silver . . . and some jewelry?" Charlotte asked, suddenly all ears and focused attention.

Rachel stopped midsentence in whatever she was discussing with Jane and whipped her head around, intent on what Charlotte had asked.

"Yes, disappeared right from on top of the buffet, silver chest and all," Joyce said. "It's getting so we'll have to lock our doors here. I've reported it to David out at the sheriff's office, and he said he'd come over with another deputy and—"

"We don't need the sheriff's office nosing around in Hopewell," Rachel said sharply. "We can—"

"Where's Susan? Are we going to start the discussion without Susan?" Jane cut in with a soft, thin voice that, nonetheless had the ability to brush aside everything else and command attention. It was times like this that Charlotte could actually believe that Jane had been a successful singer. Her voice had a "listen to me" quality to it.

"She's already over at the arts center," Joyce said, at least momentarily devoid of her concern about being murdered in her sleep. "She's having some art brought in from Philadelphia—some museum-quality pieces. She said she thought it would be good to include with the works in the art show so that folks could see how well our art stands up to the real stuff—of course she'll put your paintings between those and the others in the show, so no one is shocked by the transition from something Todd paints and something Monet paints."

Todd gave his wife a sour look, but she just returned a beatific smile, and Charlotte had the sense of a "one for Joyce" mark being slashed on her parlor wall.

"Charlotte," Grady said, "What's that you are pouring the tea from? Why it looks like a plastic Aunt Jemima pancake syrup microwavable jug."

Charlotte opened her mouth to speak, but a howl came out instead. Or, rather, in the place where she would have said something if and when she'd thought of something to say, a dog's howl rose up instead from the front lawn.

"Sam," Charlotte thought. "That husky could wake the dead with that howl."

The howl drew Jane to the parlor window.

"There's a police car over at your house, Joyce," she said. "I think your cavalry has arrived."

And with that, the weekly meeting of the book group broke up—having failed, not for the first time, to even identify, let alone open, whatever book they were supposed to be reading that week.

Chapter Three

The sighting of Officer David Burch's police cruiser on River Street, pretty much the only street in Hopewell, if you didn't count the stubby cross streets of Spring and the obligatory Penn, named after the founder of Maryland, cleared Charlotte's parlor out. Joyce and Todd were the first to go, because the police car was parked in front of their B&B. Jane and Grady followed on behind, because Hopewell was the sort of town where everyone was in everyone else's business.

Charlotte stood at the door and watched them file out suspect lineup style, and Sam squatted next to her front walk and watched them parade by.

After the exodus, Charlotte turned her attention on Sam. "What are you doing out and just sitting there for, Sam?" she said. "You know the leash ordinances here and yet you sit with a police cruiser nudged up to the curve just down the block."

Sam just looked at Charlotte and turned his head this way and that, completely nonplused at his criminal activity and how close the long arm of the law was. He did hang his tongue out, though, and started panting.

"Is that it, boy?" Charlotte asked as she descended the steps at her front door, walked out into the yard, and knelt beside the husky. "You're thirsty? That Susan doesn't take very good care of you, does she?"

Sam whined in agreement.

"Well, come on, boy, we'll see where your water bowl has gotten to."

Returning from finding the bowl, turning it over and running water in it from the spigot, and putting it down by the Wells' backdoor, where their caretaker, Susan, hopefully would find it and where Sam would be out of David Burch's sight, Charlotte returned to her front door and did a double take when she reentered her cottage.

"Rachel," she exclaimed. "You're still here." And Rachel, indeed, was still there and rocking gently in the Boston rocker.

"The deputy still over at Joyce's?" Rachel asked.

Charlotte turned and scanned the street. "It seems so. I'm surprised you aren't out there gawking with the rest of the town."

"I'm sure I'll get the complete scoop from Joyce later," Rachel said. "I told her not to bother the police on her silver—I'm with Todd on it probably just having been moved when she dusted and her mind hasn't caught up with her on what she did with it. Joyce can be a bit scatterbrained."

"Yes, well," Charlotte said as she sat down in the wing chair and poured herself a cup of now-tepid tea from the plastic syrup jug. She would have gone on to say something else, but she didn't know

16

what to say that wouldn't put her in the same stead with Rachel as the lightly dismissed Joyce. Picking the plastic jug up had reminded her that her own porcelain tea set was missing as well—and most probably because she had moved it herself without thinking about it. This was something she'd never have done in the department. This was a bad habit creeping up on her in retirement.

"What is it, Charlotte? You look concerned."

"Oh, nothing, really. I think I'm just becoming absentminded, I think. Losing my edge—and not yet out to pasture for a year."

Joyce was looking at Charlotte sharply. "Do you miss your work tremendously? Still keep a hand in it, do you? Go up to Annapolis now and again and check in the caseloads at the department?"

"Oh, no. Yes, I miss some aspects of the work, of course. Not the aggravation and the frustration of not finding solutions, of course, and not always being able to close the books. But I was ready for retirement; it's just a matter of rebuilding my interests."

Rachel relaxed visibly. "Well, you certainly have thrown yourself into those. Sailing. I cannot imagine what has possessed you to take that up so late in life."

"I've always wanted to sail," Charlotte said somewhat defensively. "But there was never time."

"Ah, the universal answer of the workaholic no longer in a demanding job. Sailing's a sport to start young if you want to be able to do it into retirement, though. And that's your local doctor's advice."

"And very good advice it is, I'm sure," Charlotte responded. "But it's different with doctors, like you, isn't it, Rachel? Never can

17

retire can you? You just move to progressively smaller towns with fewer patients to make demands on you."

"Yes, I suppose," Rachel said. She had risen from the wing chair, though, and was standing at the window and talking more to the street than to Charlotte.

"I would think that the transition was quite difficult for you," Rachel continued. "Leaving a demanding job that many would think was both exciting and gut wrenching and moving to a small hideout like Hopewell, and, on top of that, losing your husband at the same time—all of the normal props being kicked out from underneath you at one time. It would be normal for you to feel off balance—lonely and a bit vulnerable. Was your split with your husband painful?"

"Interesting that you would refer to Hopewell as a hideout, but I suppose it's a bit of that for me. I just couldn't stay where I was and disengage from my life. And I needed to. And the split from Sydney? No, not painful, I don't think—at least not for me. He always said I was more married to my job than to him. And as gruesome as my job could get, I don't naysay what he said—of the two, I preferred the job. I can clearly see that. And the divorce? I dare say that's more painful for that secretary he ran off with, Delores, now than it is for either me or Sydney. I doubt that Sydney focuses on her all that much—just a younger, sleeker model. He bought one of the fancy eye-candy sports cars at the same time, you know. I think it was a Dodge Viper or something like that. It will spend as much time in the service garage as Delores spends in the beauty parlor, and neither one of them is likely to give Sydney good service. No, I think he has gotten what he deserved.

18

And as a husband, he deserved more from me, I'll admit—so I don't bear any grudges against him."

For a moment silence reigned in the parlor, with Rachel still looking at the street through the window and Charlotte's eyes now scanning the room, inexplicably checking to see if she'd brought the Japanese tea service in here, or if something else in here was amiss—something in her brain was telling her that something was amiss, an occupational hazard of hers she hadn't grown out of yet. But having found nothing she could put her thumb on, she continued. "Well, I don't begrudge him much. An experiment gone wrong. But what about you? Have you tried marriage?"

Rachel had looked relaxed right up to that point, but when Charlotte asked that question she seemed to freeze stiff. And she didn't answer immediately. When she did speak, she said, "No, I've known all my life that men weren't for me. And the medical profession is demanding much in the same way as your career was."

"You hesitated," Charlotte said, but as soon as she'd said it she wanted to bite her lip and take it back. This career-developed nosiness and interrogation mode was another bad habit she needed to slough off in retirement, and she saw that saying that had had a negative effect on Rachel's stance. "I'm sorry, I didn't mean to say it like that. But you didn't answer directly, and I am afraid I might have struck a nerve. Are there some painful misses in your past life, perhaps?"

"No, no near misses. Just a subject I'd rather not talk about."

"Fair enough. There certainly don't seem to be any threats along those lines here in Hopewell," Charlotte said, trying to make her voice light to bring the conversation back onto a comfortable level.

Rachel turned and looked at her and visibly relaxed. "There's always our good professor, Grady. He seems to have his sights on you."

"Lord love a duck," Charlotte said, with a laugh that perhaps had just a twinge of nerves to it. "I wouldn't have Grady Tarbell on a Christmas tree. You can bet I checked the male population out before I got here. The only eligible man I've seen here is Deputy Burch, and he's young enough to be my son."

At the mention of the police deputy's name, Rachel seemed to tense up again, and she turned back to the window and looked out. Charlotte heard her sigh, and then she moved the curtain back in place that she'd held aside to look out at the street and turned and looked at Charlotte and abruptly changed the subject. "Well, if I'm going to get lunch before we have to be at the arts center for the judges' meeting, I guess I'd best shove off."

"Would you like to join me here for lunch?"

"No, thank you, Charlotte. I have some medical notes to look at while I'm eating. But thanks for the invitation."

The demur didn't sound all that convincing to Charlotte. But she didn't blame Rachel. Her lack of cooking skills had been learned quickly and well in the town. In fact, a recent survey of the residents for classes at the arts center had focused on cooking classes, and Charlotte strongly suspected this sudden interest was entirely for her benefit.

As she stood at the door to see Rachel off down the two blocks to her own house just beyond the old elementary school that had been turned into an arts center when all of the families with children had flocked off to the cities, Charlotte noticed that the police cruiser was no longer parked in front of Joyce and Todd's B&B, just one door beyond Rachel's house.

Charlotte sensed the excitement that everyone else did upon seeing David Burch's cruiser on River Street. Police cars were so prevalent in Annapolis where she'd come from that they had been almost invisible to her, but here David, the Talbot County sheriff's deputy responsible for this section of the county, was assigned to such a wide swatch of territory that he rarely came to their sleepy "artists' colony" of urban dwellers trying to make the most of their silver years.

And Charlotte hadn't wanted to crowd David in his work, so, although it was impossible not to come in contact with him occasionally in her position as the town's mayor, she thus far had worked hard to stay clear of him.

As she watched Rachel walk up the street, she felt a warm silkiness brush against her hand and looked down to see Sam's yearning eyes looking up into hers. She leaned down and scratched his ear. "Yes, I miss the Wellses too, Sam. They are good neighbors—and certainly more attentive to you than Susan is. They'll be back as soon as they've dug up Turkey, though. And, if you're good, maybe they'll bring you a mastodon bone."

Chapter Four

Charlotte, Rachel, and Jane all approached the arts center from their different directions—Rachel and Jane from their homes flanking each side of the old school building and Charlotte from farther down the street—almost like they were a precision team of marchers. This was one aspect of retirement to the river that had not yet ceased to amuse Charlotte. Everyone was still so obsessed with schedules and otherwise footloose that they arrived precisely on time for all of the activities they manufactured to make them feel useful and creative and busy.

The movement of the three was so well synchronized that they almost ran into each other where the sidewalk met the concrete walk up to the front entrance of the old school. They hadn't been looking at each other or where each of them was going. The attention of all three was focused on the old brick Manse across the street from the school—the most imposing and largest house in the village—which had sat empty, but well maintained, since long before Charlotte moved to town. It wasn't empty now. There was a moving van in front of it, which occasioned a flurry of activity and the movement of some quite elegant, and obviously very expensive furniture.

Charlotte thought that this must be some sort of festival day in Hopewell. First the visitation by Deputy Burch's police cruiser and now this. And not just this either. As she had walked up the street, Charlotte had passed a blue sedan parked on the side of the street—as discretely as any unfamiliar car could be in a town this small and out of the way. A single occupant—a dark-haired woman—was sitting in the car, and if Charlotte knew anything about surveillance work—and she had every reason to be familiar with it—this woman wasn't lost or waiting to pick up someone in the house she was sitting in front of. She was here watching someone or looking for something.

"What's that all about?" Rachel asked Charlotte, indicating the moving van.

"Why ask me?"

"You are the mayor, aren't you? Aren't you supposed to know everything new that's happening in this town?" Rachel laughed, though, to take the edge off the accusation.

"Hell, I don't even know what the woman is doing sitting in that car up the street," Charlotte said. And she too laughed. "She certainly isn't anyone from the village."

Rachel turned her eyes up the street, and a little scowl formed on her face and she seemed to withdraw upon herself.

"I think she must be moving in at last," Jane said.

Both Charlotte and Rachel turned their attention to her.

"Brenda Brandon."

"Yes, what about her?" Charlotte asked. The name was certainly familiar. That was the name of one of the leading ladies of the movies, having been one of few who had made the successful transition from bombshell to respected leading lady actress to box office mature roles. But what did this have to do with her, Charlotte wondered.

"Brenda Brandon the movie star," Jane repeated just to make sure the other two women were following her. "She owns that house, but no one has lived there for years. Now, I guess she's finally leaving Hollywood and moving in with us."

Rachel started to say something, but Jane signaled her surreptitiously—or at least it would be surreptitiously if Charlotte's powers of observation hadn't been superb—and Rachel held whatever she was going to say.

"And the woman in the car?" Charlotte asked, believing now that Jane was the font of all information, and filing the little exchange she'd seen between Jane and Rachel in the back of her mind.

"Beats me," Jane answered. "Maybe the great diva has bodyguards?"

"Doubtful," Charlotte said. "If she's still there when our meeting's over, I'll just walk up to her window and ask her what's she up to. I guess that comes under the heading of Hopewell mayoral duties."

They found Susan Purcell at the back of the gallery room, opening heavy wooden art frame boxes and removing paintings. She was such a small, slight figure of a woman that some of the cases seemed to dwarf her, but she was handling them deftly enough.

"There you are, Susan. Getting a start, I see," Charlotte said as the three women entered the large room to the left of the old school entrance hall, which had been turned into a large, airy, white-walled gallery space. Art works were already hung around on three of the four walls and on a network of partitions slicing up the center of the room. Charlotte strode out beyond the other two, who had stopped short near the entrance to take in what had already been hung. "Those aren't entered in the competition, are they?"

"No, most certainly not," Susan said with a bit of a snort. "These are real art—several McCurdles and that group of Thompsons over there—and the smaller, more delicately painted Vormeers still in the cases over here."

Susan had a way about her that seemed to set people off. She was younger than most in the village and dressed in an avant-garde style that screamed individualism. And she was bossy in a manner that insinuated she was the only one in the room with any brains. This was linked up with a whiny voice that could quickly get to you and a sharp tongue to match. She gave Charlotte the sensation of fingernails being run across a blackboard.

"And you're going to hang them all down at this end, not mingle them with the canvases entered in the show?" Charlotte asked as she moved in to help, taking up one of the smaller of the cases and examining it for clues on how she could get into it and retrieve whatever treasure was inside.

"Yes, all over here," Susan answered. "So these will be what people first see when they come into the room and won't retreat in despair from the trash at the other end." She tossed her head to flip her

25

bushy mane of raven curls back over her shoulder and closed her claws around one of Charlotte's hand. "Do mind that case, please. It's something that should be opened by experts only. These are on loan from Barnes, you know. They must be handled with extreme care."

Charlotte was about to say something, when Rachel and Jane approached. Jane looked to be in such distress that Charlotte turned her attention in that direction.

"Susan." It almost exploded from her lips. "You have my landscapes in the shadows over there, in the far corner. I thought we agreed that they would be the transition pieces to the works on loan. I—"

"Upon reflection, with everything in situ, I thought that Todd Vales abstracts would better suit," Susan answered, with just a touch of snottiness to her voice.

"Better suit? But the committee—"

"Committees are only good for pointing out the obviously unsuitable," Susan retorted. "That's why I was brought here as curator. In the available light here, which is shockingly inadequate, I agree, the Vale pieces—those by both of the Vales shine as much less insipid."

"Insipid?" Jane was almost screaming, and Rachel had to take her by the shoulders and guide her back to the other side of the room. But before she could be pulled away, Jane gave Susan a venomous look that seemed quite unlike Jane's mousy persona. Unfortunately, it was lost on Susan, who wasn't even looking. But it wasn't lost on either Charlotte or Rachel.

As Rachel dragged Jane and her clinched fists away, Susan was deftly opening the art case and pulled out a small, gilt-on-wood framed painting of an English garden that had been rendered in heavily loaded broad strokes in oils that nonetheless had captured the sense of delicate plantings of flowers backed by fully leafed trees with luminescent color that leaped off the canvas.

"A Vormeer," Susan said almost reverently. "Not as well known as the other masters of his period, but worshipped by those with the proper art education."

"Yes, it's lovely, dear," Charlotte said. "But don't you think that Jane—"

"Jane's a cow," Susan said. And that seemed to be the end of that discussion.

"Well, it will be a little hard to have our meeting now," Charlotte said. "And there doesn't really seem to be a need for a meeting if all of the decisions are made and no help is needed in organizing . . . so . . ." She was slowing down and leaving an opening for Susan to realize how pushy and dismissive she was being. But, of course, Susan didn't catch the ball on that.

"That suits me," she said. "I think I can get this in order in half the time it would take a committee. And I'm not unaccustomed to having to hold up everyone else's end."

Charlotte couldn't resist. "Well, perhaps you might hold up a bit more of an end when it comes to taking care of the Wells' husky, Sam, then, don't you think? He's out unleashed a bit more than he should be. I know that he's almost as big as you are and that walking him on a leash would be a strain, but it is, after all, a consideration we have for one another here. And he seems to be spending more time begging me to do for him than—"

"The Wellses weren't really all that clear that the house sitting came with that sort of responsibility or that their dog was so large and demanding . . . and I wasn't aware that my activities were quite your responsibility."

"Well, there is an ordinance about the keeping of dogs, and as mayor—"

"Yes, well when I've finished all of the work that everyone is leaving for me here, I'll be sure to go down to the library and study all of the ordinances of this quaint little burg. And I'll see about using a leash to walk him more."

While they had been talking, Susan had been opening the art cases and taking the paintings out.

"Can I help you get those hung?" Charlotte asked, not wanting to deepen the disagreement. The deeper it got, the less tolerable Susan was being.

"You can help by taking these cases away somewhere, but be careful of them, as we'll want to repack the paintings in them. And, here, I'll show you where they are to go." With that, Susan virtually snatched the case the Vormeer had come in out of Charlotte's hands and started walking toward a door that led to a back corridor in the old school building.

"I think I'm fully capable of finding the storage room myself," Charlotte said in a somewhat hesitant and weak voice, feeling she had to say something.

But Susan was already walking away from her, and, if she heard Charlotte's rejoinder, she made no sign that she did.

Feeling fully inadequate and unwanted, after she had taken all of the cases to the storage room, Charlotte just left by a rear exit. Hearing the lock close with a solid click behind her, Charlotte walked around to the front of the building, assuming she'd find Jane and Rachel there. But they were nowhere to be found.

Turning her nose toward home, being grateful, actually, that the meeting of the art show judges committee had fizzled but wondering where she was going to fit a retake in her busy schedule—a thought that made her laugh considering that her schedule could hardly be considered busy now—she strode off in her hallmark broad and determined steps back toward the cottage. And even though it looked like she was just ambling along, her training was not rusty, and she noticed that the car with its unfamiliar woman occupant wasn't at the curb down the street anymore—but that if she hopped to she might be in a position to save a priceless antique from oblivion.

A small sports car was parked at the curb in front of the manse where movers hustled and bustled about with assorted Chippendale and Sheraton pieces in polished cherry and mahogany, covered with rich silks and brocades. A trim woman with strikingly lustrous gray hair was bent over the car's open trunk. She was fighting with an etched-glass antique globe lamp with bronze fittings and was about to lose the battle. Charlotte moved swiftly to her aid and barely got there in time to prevent a glass globe from having an unfortunate meeting with the pavement.

"Uh, thanks," the woman said in a rich contralto. "I refused to let the movers handle this precisely because I didn't want this to happen. You saved the *Gaslight* memento."

The woman looked up and gave Charlotte, who was close in beside her, still holding one end of the lamp, a brilliant smile. She was gorgeous and Charlotte recognized her immediately.

"The *Gaslight* memento?" She asked.

"Yes, it's not really a style I'd pick, but I like to keep something from the set of each of my movies, and this is from the remake of *Gaslight*."

"Yes, I remember that well," Charlotte said. "Ingrid Bergman got an academy award for her performance in the original, but I thought you were every bit as good. So, you would be our new neighbor, Brenda—"

"Boynton," the woman completed Charlotte's sentence with an emphatic interjection. And then, when Charlotte raised her eyebrow at that, the woman continued. "Sorry, it was rude of me to interrupt. But I would like to start my new life here on a completely new foot. Brenda Brandon is my stage name, but here in Hopewell, I hope to be known by my given name, which is Boynton. I hope you don't mind."

"Certainly not. There, I think we have your lamp back up right. Would you like me to help you carry it in?"

"Oh, yes, please, if you have the time. That's quite neighborly of you. But perhaps I'm presuming. Are you a neighbor?"

"Yes, I'm Charlotte Diamond. I live just up the street there, in Diamond Cottage—or at least that's what it says on the sign in front. It's what told me I was home when I was shopping for a riverfront home on the Eastern Shore. The name reached out and told me I was where I belonged."

30

"It's a lovely little place," Brenda said, lifting her gaze to Charlotte's cottage. "And the dog in the yard is precious. A husky, is it?"

"Yes, that's Sam. But he's not mine—despite what he seems to think—he belongs to the Wellses at the house beyond mine and is being taken care of, although not all that well, by a young woman who has come here to help us establish an arts center in the old school house across the street. The Wellses are retired archaeologists who can't resist going off on expedition from time to time."

"Oh, my, there must be quite a collection of interesting people in Hopewell," Brenda said. They had reached the bottom of the brick steps up to the ornate double doors of the two-story brick colonial building, dating, it would appear, back to the eighteenth century.

"Yes, a lot of people in the arts appear to have retired here," Charlotte answered. "That isn't me, although I've only been here for about six months myself. And although I've thrown myself into trying out the classes and viewing the exhibits Susan Purcell is putting on offer at the new arts center, I'm afraid I'm miles behind everyone else here in artistic talent and ability. I just get roped into the activities because I was first roped into being mayor. Obviously no one else wanted the job, and I can be so gullible."

Charlotte only then realized that Brenda was giving her a slightly pensive expression. They were standing away from the door at the top step while two brawny movers struggled diligently at getting a Sheraton sideboard through the door without touching the wood of the obviously valuable antique against the equally obviously valuable woodwork of the door frame. Charlotte had the brief thought that she

31

certainly would have like to have these movers when she had arrived here.

"Did you say Susan Purcell?" Brenda asked.

"Yes. She's the only one who is a more recent resident of Hopewell than I am—well, I guess you are the most recently arrived—and she's only here temporarily, it would seem."

"Really? That's . . . interesting."

Charlotte, ever attuned to the slightly off utterance, was about to pursue Brenda's unusual interest in Susan, but the movers had now cleared the door, and Brenda had already turned and walked inside.

Charlotte followed her, and the vision of the entrance foyer took her breath away. The foyer was a perfect circle, a real surprise from the solid square corners and perfectly matched width and height proportions of the building from the outside. And staircases swept up both sides of the circle and met at the top in a balcony where a wide doorway led into a cross hall that, Charlotte surmised, probably led to two generously proportioned bedrooms on either side. The woodwork in the foyer was ornate, all painted a rich cream color, offsetting the maroon carpeting on the stair treads perfectly. And all was illuminated by a gigantic brass and crystal chandelier hanging from the center of a domed ceiling.

"It's breathtaking," Charlotte said. "An astonishing surprise from the angular proportions of the house from the outside."

"Thank you," Brenda responded, a sense of pride and appreciation for Charlotte's comment. "Let's bring the lamp on through to the dining room, shall we? They brought the sideboard in just now, and that might be a safe place to put the lamp for now."

Charlotte's awe was magnified as she entered the large, nearly square dining room to the right of the foyer. It was an airy room, with two tall, many-paned windows looking out onto the front lawn and two on the outer wall at the side too. A large fireplace graced the interior wall. A Sheraton dining table, which looked capable of seating twelve, was already in the center of the room, hovering over a large rolled-up oriental carpet on polished, wide-planked oak flooring. The Sheraton sideboard was on the wall against the foyer on the left as they walked in. The most breathtaking aspect of the room was the chinoiserie blue and white with green and red accent wall paper, which either must have dated back centuries or was an expert reproduction.

"This is perfect," Charlotte said. "And the furniture fits in just right too. How did you ever find this place? This is unlike anything else in the Hopewell area."

"Oh, I didn't find it," Brenda said with a gorgeous smile. "It's always been with me. I—and the furniture too, for that matter, are just coming home. This is my childhood home. I always knew I'd come back here someday, so I've kept it and paid a pretty price to keep it maintained. I guess you could say that I've grown weary of Hollywood. I wanted to come home."

Later, as Charlotte was walking up River Street to her own home, a much more modest cottage, but one that she felt suited her far better than Brenda's manse ever could, Charlotte's thoughts went back to the car, with its unfamiliar occupant, that had been parked up the street when Charlotte had gone to the arts center earlier in the afternoon. Charlotte had meant to ask Brenda if she knew anything about the woman. But it had slipped her mind. Brenda was so breathtaking in person—certainly as much as she was on camera—that all other thoughts had been thrown out of Charlotte's mind in her presence.

But, not to worry. Brenda was home now, as she termed it herself, so there would be plenty of opportunity for them to talk. And maybe the slight mystery of an unusual interloper on River Street would remain just that, a slight mystery. A mystery not needing to be solved. There was a time when Charlotte considered mysteries not needing to be solved to be a godsend.

When she reached her front steps, Sam seemed so delighted to see her that she couldn't resist sitting on the step for a few moments and petting him. She had considered getting a pet when she retired, never having had the time and patience for one while she was working. But she had never considered a dog. Cats. Cats were more independent and didn't require as much effort and attention. But looking into Sam's eyes, Charlotte could almost imagine another person in there—another being who would make her feel a little less lonely. In fact, Sam, she thought, as she gave a little laugh and Sam took that as an invitation to move his muzzle and tongue to her cheek, was probably the first man she had met that she could tolerate. All the years she'd been married to Sydney she had never lost the feeling of loneliness and separation.

But a cat, that would be much more practical.

The ringing of the telephone from inside the cottage galvanized Charlotte into motion. She hefted her bulk up onto her feet with a woof that perked Sam's ears up in its familiarity to his language and entered the house—but not in time to beat the whirring of the message machine and her own voice announcing she wasn't there.

34

When Charlotte heard who it was who was calling, she just let the machine take the message. In a rather accusing voice Susan was reminding Charlotte that the judges' committee for the art contest was supposed to have met that afternoon and now would be expected to meet at 9:00 sharp the next morning—that Susan couldn't be expected to do all of the work on the art show herself.

Later, as Charlotte sat alone in her parlor, having picked up a book because nothing on television enticed her and now finding that the book didn't particularly engage her mind tonight either, it struck Charlotte to question why she was picking up all of these activities in her retirement. The answer didn't give her comfort. She wasn't ready to wind down to barely breathing. She missed her job, even if she had been burned out when she retired. She missed the activity and, yes, the excitement. And she felt so unfulfilled. Only her job had given her anything close to the feeling of fulfillment. She was loading up with activities because she didn't want to face up to the fact that she was lonely and had been lonely most of her life—and that she'd never really felt contentment.

A cat. That's what she needed. She wondered where Sam was this evening. If Susan had left him out—or had bothered to feed him or made sure his water dish was filled. The Wellses had always taken such good care of him—and he'd rarely been left out, certainly not on his own, unleashed, in the few months the Wellses had been here after Charlotte had moved in.

Charlotte smiled at the memory of how happy he'd been to see her coming up the walk to the cottage this afternoon and the joy he'd exhibited when she stopped to give him some attention. But a cat. That was probably as much as Charlotte could cope with. And maybe not even that. She had planned to do some traveling in her retirement. That was hard to do with either a cat or dog. And a bird was messy and out of the question anyway. And fish were no answer to boredom.

It was really too early to turn in, but Charlotte was bored—and lonely—and the solution to both of these had long been just to go to sleep and close the world out. On that basis, she was getting a terrific amount of sleep these last six months. At least now she didn't have the nightmares she tended toward when she was working—when the sordidness and cruelty of the world of her profession intruded even into her sleeping moments. But at least those weren't boring. Now, she was afraid, she was sinking into boredom.

In the middle of the night, Charlotte was awakened by the howling of a dog. It sounded like Sam. She felt tears in her eyes, thinking how similar Sam's mournful howling was to what she felt like doing herself. Sam and her—both lonely and left out on their own. She squeezed her eyes tight and willed herself into sleep, aided by an eerie silence that followed the ending of the plaintive cry of the distant dog in the night.

Chapter Five

It had rained sometime in the night, which had brought up the smell of pine on the morning breeze, and Charlotte sat out on her screened porch off the back of the cottage and savored her coffee and toast while watching the river. It was the promise of mornings like this that had enticed her to retire near the water. For all the years she lived in Annapolis, with its many coves and access to the Bay via the Severn River, she had never had the privilege of living on the water but, rather, had lived in a small, but cozy old townhouse near the Statehouse.

It was still early when she was finished with her breakfast, and she moved to the front door to retrieve the morning paper. She'd moved to the lazy side of the state, but she wasn't ready to give up her news yet, so she was one of the few residents of Hopewell who received daily delivery of the Baltimore *Sun*. And then there was the local free paper that would appear on her doorstep each morning whether she wanted it or not.

She could see, though, when she opened the front door, that it would be a while before she'd be able to read the *Sun*—and that she'd have to read it outside—because she discovered a wet and muddy-pawed Sam curled up on top of it in the center of the brick walk from the street to her door. The local paper was nowhere to be found, which wasn't all that surprising, as delivery times for that were erratic.

"Where have you been, Sam?" Charlotte asked, as he lifted his head dreamily, fighting to raise himself up from sleep and gave her a loving smile. "And what have you got around your neck?"

Charlotte leaned down to find that Sam was attached to his leash still. Charlotte thought this was strange—not just that a dog Susan had let run free was wearing a leash, but also that if she'd taken him out on the leash, why had she left it on him? Charlotte didn't want to criticize as it was an indication that Susan was trying to do the right thing—but leaving him out with a leash on his neck? Really. He could snag it on something and choke himself.

Charlotte took one end of the leash, and Sam raised up and followed her—quite willingly—as, in her robe and slippers, she marched across the still-wet grass between her cottage and the Wells' house and rapped on the front door. She was in the mood to give Susan a dressing down for her neglect of the dog and was fully prepared to tell her that she was going to report the treatment to the Wellses, even if they were in Turkey and not really able to do much about it—and she intended to carry through with the threat, if need be.

But there was no answer to her knocking. And there was no answer either when Charlotte moved around to the back door. Being who she was—and not the least because she was tall enough to look inside them, Charlotte went around the walls of the house to look into the interior through the windows that weren't covered with curtains—but there was no sign of Susan inside.

She reasoned that Susan must have gotten an early start for the arts center. It was still more than an hour before they were to meet there, but Susan likely had other work to do there as well.

Looking down at the food and water bowls at the back door, Charlotte could see that both were empty. She wondered how long it had been since Sam had eaten. She asked him that very question, but he just cocked his head and lolled his tongue out and wagged his tail at her.

She decided not to assume he'd been taken care of this morning, so she filled his water bowl from the spigot and, while he was lapping at that, she went back into the cottage and decided to sacrifice the half of steak she'd saved from a meal two days earlier and took that out and put it in his food bowl. The way he leaped on that indicated to her that he hadn't eaten in a while either. And he looked a fright with his muddy paws and wet fur.

"Where have you been, boy?" She asked again. The look he gave her—the gratitude he showed for the food she'd brought him—tore at her heart. Charlotte returned to the cottage and changed into work clothes. Then she went into her basement and pulled out a large galvanized metal tub she had there and some old towels and dragged the tub out to the grass between the two houses. Unreeling the hose at the back of her house, she started filling the tub while wondering whether she had soap that would suit and trying to think of where she had put the sponge she used to wash her car. This might make her late to the meeting at the arts center, but she'd just use it as a teeing-off point for what she had to say to Susan about the care she wasn't taking of Sam. And she certainly hoped that if Susan was inside her house, she'd come to the window and get an eye full of Charlotte doing what she should have done.

For the next half hour, she fought with Sam in the tub—not because Sam didn't enjoy having a bath—but because he enjoyed it too much. The process of drying him was even more of a hassle than washing him had been.

When Charlotte was finished, she brought Sam and his bowls in on her back screened porch, deciding that one way or the other, his free-roaming days would be curtailed. Then she took her time showering and dressing for the meeting herself. She was going to be late, but that was fine with her. She wanted to get Susan's attention. With the people Charlotte had worked with in the previous nearly forty years, Susan didn't stand a chance against her—and Charlotte decided it was time to stop using velvet gloves in dealing with the unpleasant young woman.

Charlotte's ire and resolve dissolved the minute she stepped into the gallery at the arts center. Although she was a good forty-five minutes late, Susan wasn't there yet. But Rachel and Jane were there, and both seemed just as happy as not that Susan wasn't there.

"The place was locked tight when we arrived nearly simultaneously," Rachel said. "Luckily Jane has a key." Jane and Rachel lived on either side of the building, and it had been Charlotte's suggestion when the arts center first opened that at least one of them should have a key to the place in case of emergencies.

"Susan wasn't here, so we went ahead and did a preliminary scan of the paintings and have agreed between us on awards—subject, of course, to your concurrence," Jane said, rather smugly. "Since Susan isn't here, her votes can just not count as long as you agree with our selections."

Charlotte knew she should feel a bit put out that the two of them had moved ahead with the judging, but, truth be known, she had dreaded the responsibility to pick. She knew practically nothing about art.

"Whatever you two have decided is fine with me," Charlotte said. "As long as you have agreed. And, Jane, I'm sorry about yesterday. I know you didn't enter your artwork in the competition purely because you had been promised that your paintings would be grouped with those on loan from the art museum. I think that Susan—"

"Oh, I've taken care of Susan," Jane said. The flash of malice in the woman's eyes set Charlotte back on her heels a bit. This wasn't the Jane Charlotte had come to know. But perhaps she had such a pride in her art that it brought out the assertiveness in her. Charlotte did think that Jane's art must be very good; it sold in the Annapolis art galleries. Even to Charlotte's untrained eye, it certainly looked a lot more professional than anything Charlotte had seen being produced in art class, with the possible exception of Todd Vale's paintings. His were entirely different from her romanticized landscapes, though—much more brash and full of bold color. And certainty abstract to the point that Charlotte wouldn't have know which side was up.

Charlotte started to ask for an explanation of Jane's comment, but Rachel cut in with a, "Well, let's show you what we've decided and

41

then, unless you don't agree with our picks, we can all go home again before Susan arrives and spoils what's left of our morning."

Charlotte had to give Jane credit for being evenhanded. Despite Susan's obvious preference of place for Todd Vale's work, Jane and Rachel had selected two of his for awards, including for the "Best of Show" category.

Sharing Rachel's sentiment that they would be just as happy to avoid the arrival of Susan—and having lost steam on her determination to dress the woman down here and now about her treatment of Sam— Charlotte quickly concurred with all of Rachel and Jane's selections and the three were on their way. Jane locked up again as they finished, and the two women were already entering Rachel's house to share a cup of coffee that Charlotte had begged off of when Charlotte remembered that she was going to ask Jane what she meant by having taken care of Susan. If Jane had actually thought of something that would work in that department, Charlotte thought she could use some pointers on what to use on Susan herself.

Charlotte walked back up River Street and when she got to her cottage, she squared her shoulders and walked on to the Wells' house. Once more, though, there was no answer when she knocked on both the front and rear doors. The only greeting she got was an enthusiastic "come play with me" greeting from Sam when she walked between the two houses and he spotted her from his imprisonment on her screened porch.

Perplexed, Charlotte walked back to the detached single-car garage at the rear of the Wells' property almost abutting the tidal wall they'd had built at the river's edge only to have her perplexity expanded when she saw that Susan's compact car was in the garage. Susan was somewhere in the village, but Charlotte was certainly at a loss where that could be. Susan hadn't exactly made friends here, it seemed, other than with the Vales. She would call them to see if Susan might be there.

Returning to the cottage, Charlotte rang the Vales, but they didn't pick up either. Perhaps the three of them had gone into Easton or Cambridge for the day, Charlotte thought.

And then Charlotte decided she was tired of thinking. She went out on the porch and enjoyed the company of Sam for a few minutes—company that was mutually appreciated—and then she decided that since the meeting at the arts center hadn't taken near the time she thought it would that the day was too beautiful to waste—she's take the Penguin out again for a spin on the river before lunch. As she dressed for boating, she laughed at the thought of taking the Penguin for a spin. She was probably, she thought, the only one on the river who could literally spin a Penguin, however unintentionally.

Chapter Six

Charlotte was out in the middle of the Choptank, her little Penguin revolving around and around in the river, having a mind of its own, when she struck the other boat. Right before that she had done something with the sail that righted the little sailboat and changed its course into a straight line, but she didn't have time to do any more than trumpet a victorious "There you go" before she looked up and saw a blur of color and a startled face as she plowed into the side of a sleek Laser sailboat.

Charlotte heard the explicative and splash as the other sailor went over the side of the Laser.

At that moment, Charlotte changed from struggling whale in a teaspoon to first responder. Pushing her conscious thoughts aside and letting her instincts take over, she neatly turned the Penguin and hove back around to the side of the Laser and, being careful not to overdistribute her weight, first grabbed the bow rope of the Laser, which thankfully had not capsized in the collision, with one hand to keep it from drifting off and then brought it around to help the other in lifting a sputtering figure from the water and hauling the waterlogged Laser sailor into the Penguin.

With a jolly laugh, Brenda Boynton brushed strands of wet hair from her face and sputtered out a, "Well done. And to think I was sailing over to help stop you from turning those circles."

"I'm so sorry," Charlotte responded. "I'm a menace. I need to put out a flag calling off all other sailors from the Choptank when I'm riding the seas."

"You did that last maneuver smartly."

"That was lesson one at sailing school, and I hope now never to forget it again: train, train, train, and then let your instincts take over."

Charlotte looked at Brenda with mixed emotions of admiration and envy. Why, she's beautiful even when half drowned, Charlotte thought.

As if she'd read Charlotte's thoughts, Brenda gingerly sat up in the Penguin, brushed wet strands of hair from her face, and took the rope holding her Laser back. As quick as she'd been pulled into the Penguin, she was deftly preparing to transfer into the other vessel— which she did with a grace that gave rise to Charlotte's envy again.

Once Brenda was back in her boat, she turned and, with one of those winning smiles that she seemed to have such a large fund of, said, "I guess it's right back to the house for me and a shower and a shampoo."

"I'm so sorry for dumping you in the drink," Charlotte said. "And I'm doubly contrite because I know you were only coming over

45

to try to help me from my blundering efforts. I only wish there was something I could do to make it up to you."

"There is. Do you have luncheon plans?"

"Not that I know of. I sort of thought it would be dark before I could get this tub pointed back at my dock."

"As you say, let your instincts take over. You did fine after the collision. How about giving me an hour and a half to wring myself out and counter the contamination of the river, and then you can take me to lunch in Easton—if you know of a good place to eat there. I wanted to go browsing through the antique stores there today. I didn't bring nearly enough furniture to make the house feel livable."

"There's a restaurant in the Tidewater Inn—the Hunter's Tavern—and recently renovated. I've been meaning to check that out. Would that do?"

"The Tidewater Inn's still open?" Brenda asked. And then she laughed her tinkling laugh. "That should do fine. That would put us right in the heart of the antique market."

As Brenda expertly turned the laser and set its sails to take her back to the dock at her house, as imposing a view from the river from this distance as it was from the street, Charlotte couldn't help but note that her spirits had lifted a mile following this little accident. Brenda Boynton conveyed contentment and had a pleasant effect on her that all of the art and literary activities Charlotte had engaged in since moving to Hopewell hadn't managed.

* * * *

Easton, almost due north of Hopewell on the Choptank, and itself located on the Tred Avon with access to the Chesapeake Bay, was

46

the county seat and the nearest town of any size. An eighteenth-century fishing village, it now was one of the gateways to the bayside resorts and a cultural center for the well-heeled Eastern Shore crowd. The Tidewater Inn, big and square and plopped down right in the middle of town, had been a high-pamper getaway target for travelers for nearly two hundred and fifty years.

The cozy, warm-wood paneling and low ceiling of the inn's Hunter's Tavern proved a perfect spot for Charlotte and Brenda to let their hair down and become better acquainted. As they talked, they each spoke with some intimacy about their quite disparate careers and the conversation was maintained at a comfortable pace, aided by each showing more interest in the work of the other than in trumpeting their own success and importance, to the point that they were delving more deeply into their personal lives than either probably realized they were doing.

"That's how I often felt too," Brenda was saying, "in the center of a scene shoot, all lights and cameras and attention on me, but feeling alone, so totally alone."

"Alone?" Charlotte said with a bit of shock in her voice. "Alone in a crowd of adoring fans."

"Yes, just like you were just saying about your own work."

"Was I? Did I say I was lonely even while in the center of the action? Yes, yes, I guess I did. I'm sorry, I've rambled so, and I'm sure I've bored you to death with my work stories."

"Oh, no. I'm finding them fascinating. As you've talked I've compared how we movie people portray people like you, and I find our attempts pitiful and far less exciting than reality. You should consult for the movies." And when Charlotte chuckled at that suggestion, Brenda laid her hand on Charlotte's forearm as it rested on the table top and, not seeing Charlotte blush at that small intimacy, reiterated. "You really should. I know of several producers who would snap your services up in an instant."

Charlotte was discombobulated at this suggestion, never in her wildest dreams ever considering doing such a thing, and she strove to move the spotlight back on Brenda. She felt she was getting very close to monopolizing the discussion, and, aware of the balance that had made their lunch so pleasant and the exchange so free flowing, she fought to hang onto that mood. This was the best time she'd had since moving to Hopewell.

"Your work sounds so rewarding that I'm surprised you could pull yourself away from it. You obviously are in demand—one of the few women box office guarantees, according to the smattering of articles I've read on the movies—and you've had no trouble moving to mature roles—not that you're old of course."

Brenda laughed. "Old is certainly preferable to sweet sixteen— and I'm sure you agree," she said. Her laugh had sounded a bit hollow, though, and Charlotte looked sharply at her and was able to discern the flash of pain in her eyes.

"I'm sorry. Did I tread too hard on your privacy?"

"No, no, not at all." There was a pause and then Brenda continued. "No, you haven't. It's good to be able to talk about these things with someone. I left because of the isolation and loneliness. I'm not sure why I thought it would be any better in Hopewell, which isn't exactly the center of the universe. But it's home—or was at one time. I didn't really think. I guess I was in retreat."

"In retreat?" Charlotte asked.

"Yes, if I'm honest, I guess that's a good thing to call it. I had a friend . . . the one person who could make me forget the isolation and loneliness of center stage."

"Such a friend is a godsend," Charlotte said, feeling envious, as she had never had such a friend—at least, maybe, not until now. "That friend is gone from you now?"

"Yes, yes she is. Have you ever heard of Helga Lund, the costume designer?"

"Helga Lund? Yes, I've heard of her in some context. Movies, of course, but there was something . . . else." Charlotte's musings ground to a halt as she remembered the something else. "Wasn't she . . . didn't she die some months back. A questionable death. Found hanging from a chandelier, wasn't it?"

Then Charlotte looked up and saw the sudden devastation in Brenda's face. Suddenly Brenda was no longer young and effervescent. And it was time for Charlotte to say "I'm sorry" again, something that she was painfully aware that she'd had to say to Brenda too many times already today.

"Yes, she died. In my . . . in our . . . home. I stayed around until all hope was gone to continue believing that she hadn't done that to herself. And then the house, Hollywood, all of California—the whole West Coast culture—was too fake, too cloying, too much for me to bear, and I came . . . home."

"If I'd known, I wouldn't have . . ."

49

"No, it's all right, really it is. She died . . . that way. That cannot be erased or denied. I just don't know why. We'd been so happy. If she took her own life, I cannot understand. . . . And if she didn't, if someone else took it, I am angry . . . but equally in the dark and powerless. But. . . . Well, that's that, and so I came home—retreated to Hopewell—to the familiar."

"The familiar? But surely there isn't anything in Hopewell that's familiar to you anymore—other than most of the buildings and the memories."

"Oh, you'd be surprised. Hopewell is a small town. Some things never change. And some people stay and some, like me, come back."

"There are some long-term residents in the town?" Charlotte asked. This was a revelation to her. "I thought we were all retreads from the city—come there in search of the idyllic waterside life and artistic inspiration—and to escape someplace—something—else."

"Well, those needn't be mutually exclusive," Brenda answered, her million-dollar smile back in place now. "Some, like Joyce Purcell, came back—and did so because of the pull of the idyllic life you mentioned, and . . ."

"Joyce Purcell? You don't mean . . . ?"

"Ah, yes, I guess you only know her as Joyce Vale. She was Joyce Purcell when we grew up together in Hopewell. That B&B she's running with her husband is the old Purcell place. She inherited it and she and her husband turned it into that small hotel."

"Interesting. But the name Purcell. Susan Purcell, the arts center curator. She isn't . . . ?"

"Yes, she's Joyce's daughter. But then I assumed you'd sleuthed all of that out already . . . with your background and all. I had no idea you didn't know."

"No I didn't," Charlotte said somewhat in amazement. She must have been slipping more than she thought, was what was racing through her mind. Not more than six months off the job and she was missing little details like that.

"Yes, it was quite a scandal at the time," Brenda was continuing on. "Susan wasn't married—and never did marry the father—both of which were the stuff that real scandals were made of in this part of the Eastern Shore at the time. Her father was mayor and ran the only insurance agency around, and they were supposed to be the standard setters. And yet Susan made no bones that she was going to go it alone and be a single mother. And that with the father, one of the school's new, young school teachers—a scandal in its own right—Grady, living right across town."

"Grady? Now you are losing me."

"Grady. Grady Tarbell. The baby's father. Grady's one who just stayed here—in spite of all of the tongue wagging. So some just stay put and some come back. And . . . why are you looking so perplexed, Charlotte? You didn't know? But then I guess you wouldn't know about Grady if you didn't know about Joyce and Susan either."

Charlotte's head was spinning, and she remembered little of the rest of the conversation, except that they were still chattering amiably when they had been launched out of the tavern door and Brenda was snatching familiar landmarks in Easton from her memory banks and taking Charlotte's arm comfortably in hers and guiding her to the head of Goldsborough Street for their leisurely prowl down the row of antique shops they found lining that street.

It was in the third shop they entered that Charlotte discovered that her powers of observation and remembrance hadn't atrophied as much as she was beginning to think they had.

"Interested in stamps?" the proprietor asked as he noticed Charlotte closely examining the pages of a stamp album she'd found resting on his counter. She had taken a pad of paper and a pen out of her purse and was taking some notes.

"Umm mmm," she murmured as the man hovered over her.

"Those there are particularly rare. Interwar German stamps. You can see where zeros were added after the stamp was cast—and then more added again. Inflation was so rampant in Europe at the time that prices changed astronomically even before goods could get to market. Not really in keeping with the theme of my store. But I just couldn't resist acquiring it."

"And can you tell me how you acquired it?" Charlotte said, lifting her head and looking at him and trying not to convey the question as being as important as it was.

"Well, I got it from Stan King over at King's Antiques. It really wasn't in keeping with his store at all, and he didn't fully understand the worth of the stamps. He said he'd gotten it fairly recently—not from someone living in Easton, though."

"King's Antiques?" Charlotte asked. She was looking beyond the window of the shop, trying to locate the other store.

"Yes, but he's closed today. Has gone to an auction over near the Delaware shore I think. If you're interested in the stamps—"

"I'm more interested in the engraved initials stamped on the cover of the album, I think," Charlotte said. "That does look like a G and a T to you, doesn't it?"

Charlotte was ever delighted and surprised at the serendipitous nature of life. She and Brenda had just been talking about Grady Tarbell at lunch. And here, if Charlotte's keen sense of detection hadn't gone awry, very likely was the stamp album that Grady had recently said was missing from the desk in his study.

* * * *

As they entered the realm of Hopewell on their return from Easton Charlotte and Brenda, were still bantering back and forth on whether Brenda, who had driven them in her sports car and even argued with Charlotte over the luncheon check, was going to give Charlotte curb delivery at her cottage even though Charlotte lived only steps beyond Brenda, when the argument became moot. There were three police cars and a rescue squad vehicle parked in front of Brenda's house and a gaggle of townspeople gathered around in a semicircle almost in the center of the street. Brenda parked at the curb by the wooded vacant lot next to her house and they both climbed out of the low-riding convertible with their eyes on the approaching deputy sheriff, David Burch. There was an older, and slightly more heavy set uniformed officer limping along behind him.

"Hello, Ms. Diamond," David said respectfully and took off his hat to emphasize his good manners. "And would you be Brenda Brandon?" he asked as his eyes shifted to Brenda.

"Brenda Boynton. I go by my given name here," Brenda said, as she put out a hand to welcome him. "What seems to be the problem here, Officer? I hope nothing's wrong with the house."

Charlotte had taken the moment of this introduction to look beyond the two officers at the semicircle of gathered residents. Her antenna for something dreadfully wrong was up, and her quick mind flashed back to this morning when Sam was sitting at her front door attached to his leash and she hadn't been able to locate Susan Purcell even at a meeting Susan herself had scheduled.

The townspeople were in three general clusters, with two outriders, both of who looked quite nervous and reluctant to be there. Jane Cranford and Rachel Sharp were standing near the center of the group and almost on the other side of the street. The town clerk, Mary Miller and her husband, Walt, were standing with Jane and Rachel. Jane looked like she was quaking, and Rachel, stalwart town doctor, had her arms around the slighter woman. The Vales were standing right next to the curb and closest to where Brenda had parked. Joyce was almost in hysterics and Todd was holding her tight, preventing her from plunging into the woods of the vacant lot. Grady Tarbell was the farthest away, nearly beyond Brenda's house. He looked extremely uncomfortable, and Charlotte's heart went out to him if this tableau represented what she was afraid it did. He was as isolated and spurned from his daughter's life now as he ever had been.

There were a few other village residents in yet another grouping, and Charlotte was surprised at how many were in town on the afternoon of a weekday. It struck her once again how much of a retirement village this was. The pastor of the Episcopal chapel, the only church in town, Don Dunkel, was moving from group to group, doing what pastors always seemed to be doing in these circumstances.

The greatest surprise was seeing a woman standing across the street and closer to the entry to the town than where Brenda had parked. She was a tall, unusually severe-looking woman in a plain cotton frock and what looked like muddy combat boots. The shock, though, was that Charlotte seemed to recognize her—and although Charlotte didn't know who she was and didn't remember seeing her around in town, for some reason the association she surfaced in Charlotte's mind was not just distasteful—it was evil. Charlotte couldn't place her, but she had every confidence that at some point the woman would click in her mind—and that Charlotte wouldn't be pleased when she remembered the connection.

"Not at the house, Ms. Boynton," David Burch was saying when Charlotte's attention returned to the two uniformed men standing in front of her. "This here's the Talbot County sheriff, Haws Wainwright. Haws, the owner of the house here, Ms. Boynton, . . . and Ms. Charlotte Diamond."

The sheriff came around from behind David and shook both women's hands. "Does this lot belong to you Mrs. Boynton?"

"Yes, yes it does. It's been in my family for years," Brenda answered. "What's wrong, Sheriff? Has something happened?"

"I'm afraid so," The sheriff answered. "This afternoon boaters found a body—that of a young woman—in the marshy shallows by this lot. The medical examiner is in there now." Then he turned to Charlotte. "Ms. Diamond, would you mind accompanying me into the crime scene?"

"Charlotte?" Brenda said just as Charlotte was saying "Me?"

"Yes, please, if you'll indulge us, we certainly could use your help."

"My help?" Charlotte said.

"Of course. You don't think, I hope, that the celebrated chief of the criminal investigations division of the FBI's Maryland office could move into my county without me knowing about it—and not be someone I wouldn't want to consult, retired or otherwise."

Charlotte sighed and gave a pained expression, both of which were belied by the fierce beating of her heart and the ever-familiar excitement of the hunt, dormant for six months, which rose inside her.

The sheriff and David turned and walked along the curb toward where there was a path into the wooded lot at the corner of Brenda's yard. Charlotte followed him, and Brenda moved in that direction behind them as well.

As they passed the Vale's, Joyce reached out with her hand and clutched at Charlotte's arm, and cried out, "It's Susan, isn't it. I knew it."

Hearing this cry, Jane started wailing from across the street, "It's her, I knew it. I didn't . . . I didn't. I know I said I'd taken care of her—but I just meant I'd complained about her to the arts council that sent her here."

David Burch broke off and headed for Jane, no doubt speculating that a confession of some sort might be in the offing, and Charlotte might have followed except for the clutching hand on her arm.

"Again. Just like before," Joyce growled. She looked like a crazy woman.

"What do you mean 'like before?'" Charlotte asked, trying to use as soothing a voice as she could.

"Ask her," Joyce spat out, casting her eyes beyond Charlotte's shoulder. "Ask Brenda. She returns and it happens again."

Charlotte turned to Brenda, who had tears in her eyes.

"My mother," Brenda said. "She died there, at the water's edge. When I was in high school. That's why we didn't develop the lot. That's why I left here as soon after high school as I could and only now came back. And they never found out how it happened."

Charlotte turned and embraced Brenda, but Rachel was there now, having left Jane to David and moved up to talk in guarded tones with Sheriff Wainwright a bit off to the side.

"Here, Charlotte," Rachel said gently. "I'll see to Joyce. The sheriff is waiting for you."

Charlotte's eyes darted this way and that as she entered the woods, already back in the investigator mode, already keen to find anything amiss, anything that would help solve this conundrum.

She didn't see anything of interest as they approached the river's edge, but then she saw enough to pique her interest and get her adrenaline going in high gear.

Crouching over the body as the medical examiner pulled the sheet from the dead woman's face, Charlotte looked up at the sheriff and said, "This isn't who everyone back on the street thinks it is. This isn't Susan Purcell?"

"Interesting," the sheriff said. "Do you have any idea who it is?"

"No," Charlotte answered. "It's no one who lives here, I'm pretty sure. But I have seen this woman before. She was sitting out in a car on the street yesterday. It occurred to me at the time that she was engaging in surveillance. But beyond that I have no idea. That was the only other time I saw her, and when I returned from the meeting I was going to—when I thought I'd talk to her—she was gone."

"Can you describe the car?"

"Yes, certainly. I can even give you a partial on the license plate."

"Ah, old habits," the sheriff said. But he didn't say it to criticize. He said it almost in awe, having the greatest deal of respect for the reputation of this woman.

Charlotte barely heard him, though. She was thinking back to her statement that this wasn't the woman everyone out on the street expected it to be. She knew it was quite possible that she had misspoken. She knew that it was highly likely that at least one person standing out there on River Street knew exactly who this young woman was.

Chapter Seven

"I'm sorry, Charlotte. If you've come to see Joyce, I'm afraid you are out of luck. I've just now gotten her to sleep. The sedative Rachel provided took quite some time to set in. Finding out that the murdered woman wasn't Susan was a shock in itself. There's still Susan. She's still missing. So, thanks for dropping by, but—"

"I'm sure you can help me as well as Joyce could, Todd," Charlotte said coolly, "and I believe you are aware that I'm not operating in a neighborly capacity any more—that I've been officially attached to this case now."

"Yes, we weren't aware that we had such a famous detective among us." Todd said it somewhat sourly, which was an attitude that had Todd written all over it, so Charlotte didn't mince words in responding.

"Nor did you or Joyce bother to tell me that Susan was Joyce's daughter despite all of us living on the same street. And that would bring me here as much as official duty. Susan's disappearance drops some neighborhood responsibility in my lap. I've been left with the

59

Wells' dog, which Susan is supposed to be taking care of, parked on my lawn—or, rather on my screened porch, because I have the sense of community responsibility to not leave it running free—as Joyce's daughter did. Now, since I *am* here on police business, perhaps you will invite me inside so we aren't discussing all of this in public. I can see curtains pulled aside in windows all up and down the street."

"I suppose. Yes, do come on in," Todd said reluctantly, cowed by Charlotte's majestic presence and bearing if by nothing else. He stood aside, and Charlotte sailed into the parlor and made sure that she lowered her bulk into the most substantial chair therein.

"I have a couple of questions you could help me with, actually," Charlotte opened with. "First, since Joyce is Susan's mother, it would save me time and effort to receive permission to enter the Wells' house to see if anything there would help us find her. There's no reason to think her disappearance and the body found on the lot across the street are linked—but without evidence to the contrary there's no reason not to link them, either. I could contact the Wellses for permission, but I would have to track them down in Turkey."

Todd hesitated, and Charlotte wondered why. It occurred to her for the first time, which she would return to in her thoughts, that there might be some reason why Joyce and Todd weren't quick to permit someone to look into Susan's affairs—something that might even explain why Joyce had never mentioned that Susan was her daughter. She decided to zing him.

"What if Susan is in the house? What if she has fallen and needs help? Have you or Joyce gone there to make sure that's not the case?"

"Oh, no. We didn't even think of that possibility." Todd was all flustered now, and Charlotte's trained eye told her that his reaction was genuine. She had actually played her fears of what might be the case down. The Wells house wasn't large and Charlotte had been all around it on the previous day, giving every opportunity for Susan to call out if she was in there and conscious—and she hadn't seen anything amiss through the ground-floor windows. Although Charlotte considered the possibility that she was in there, her years of training told her that what was to be found might be much more grisly than a fall down the stairs.

"Yes, yes, of course," Todd said, now all willingness to help. "Anything to help in finding Susan. I'm sure Joyce has a key to the house. I'll just—"

"No need for that. I have a key myself—that the Wellses gave me. But I want to do all of this properly. I have a form here for you to sign, if you will, giving permission."

While Todd leaned over the coffee-table to sign the paper, Charlotte asked him several questions about whether he knew of anything that would help explain Susan's absence, and, since he couldn't, if he'd have Joyce contact her if she could be any more helpful—which he said he would.

"I'll talk to Joyce later myself, when she feels up to it," Charlotte said, "and if we haven't found Susan in the meantime. It could be that she just went off on a whim for a couple of days, but that doesn't seem likely as she had arranged a meeting at the arts center not long before she went missing."

"Will that be all?" Todd replied, obviously keen for her to leave. "I had planned on cleaning out the gutters this afternoon. Now, it looks like rain, so I'll have to do it another time." He said it as if it was Charlotte's fault that it had clouded up and started to sprinkle intermittently since she had appeared on his porch.

"No, there's one other thing you could help me with. There was a woman in the crowd out in front of Brenda's house yesterday. Standing apart from the others and across the street, closer to the entrance to the village than the others were standing. She looked familiar to me, but I couldn't identify her. Do you remember seeing her and know who she is?"

"That could have been Mrs. Smith. Edith Smith," Todd answered after giving it a bit of thought. "She's reclusive—and a bit eccentric, I've heard."

"Edith . . . Smith. Rather an innocuous name. And is she a long-term resident? Despite supposedly being mayor here, I'm only recently becoming aware of how long some have lived here—and," Charlotte dug in with a sharp look at Todd, "how intertwined some of their lives are."

Todd reddened up, but he didn't venture a retort. "She's only been here five or six years. A widow, I understand. She lives at the Clagett farm just outside the village. The Clagetts were here for generations and all died out, I think. I'm not aware that she has any connection to them. Why do you ask?"

"I'm not sure. My mind is just telling me that it might be important. As I said, she seems quite familiar to me, and my brain is connecting her with something that tells me could connect with the events here of the last couple of days."

"Why don't you just go out and talk to her then?" Todd asked.

"I just might do that," Charlotte said as she worked her way out of the overstuffed chair and got to her feet. "I might do some checking first, though," she said without revealing that whenever she could avoid it, she didn't go asking questions without already knowing what the answers were. "With what little I've got to run on now," she continued, "I'm not sure what I'd even ask her. But for now, I will take a look in the Wells' house. If I find anything I think you should know about, I'll let you know. And I also have to feed Sam—something I'd like to discuss with Susan when she finally pops up. Luckily, Brenda and I stopped at a pet store in Easton yesterday and I bought some dog food. Otherwise, thanks to Susan, Sam would be one hungry and neglected puppy now."

Todd was thoroughly cowed as Charlotte sailed through the foyer and out onto the front porch and scanned the houses up and down the street for the reward of seeing curtains ruffle at the windows.

Ah, the comfort of small town living, she thought as she steamed up the street between raindrops to feed Sam and then get into the Wells' house. She was itching to see what was inside. As she walked and felt a dozen eyes follow her, though, she was slightly discontent that her cover had been blown. The locals had known she worked in the government before coming here—and she'd mentioned to Rachel that it was in a police investigative capacity—but now they knew the depth and extent of her involvement, and she felt she never again would be able to pass as simply a local, disinterested retiree.

63

Sam taken care of, with several more minutes taken in walking him and giving some attention enjoyed by dog and human alike, Charlotte descended on the Wells' house like a clipper in full sail. She felt guilty that she wasn't going to the house as quickly as possible, but she felt a responsibility to Sam too—and she knew he was a completely innocent bystander to whatever was going on.

Her fears—and, frankly her assumption—were fulfilled, although not as drastically as she thought they might be, when she got into the house. There was no aura about it of an intended departure. There was no evidence of Susan in the flesh, however, which was both a relief and a deepening of the mystery surrounding her absence. Charlotte did a cursory, but expert inventory of the signs and timeline of Susan's last presence here. Papers from the last two days, including the morning Susan was to meet Charlotte and the other art judges at the arts center, were on the front stoop—something that Charlotte hadn't noticed on that day, but then she remembered that her own local newspaper hadn't been delivered until the afternoon—something that deliverymen certainly wouldn't be permitted to do in Annapolis, but that seemed to be tolerated here in the hinterlands. The dishes in the drain board were more evidently from a dinner than a breakfast. The living areas of the first floor were in somewhat of a comfortable disarray, which indicated that Susan hadn't left on any intentional journey of any length. TV programs for the evening before last were circled on the TV guide on the coffee-table in front of the television, giving the impression that Susan had planned to be watching television that night.

Upstairs was even more revealing, and it was here that the mystery deepened and Charlotte began to link up some threads—which always was the beginning of the end in her investigations. There was no evidence that Susan's closet was stripped of clothes and an apparently full, matched set of women's luggage was lurking at the back of the walk-in closet. Lingerie and blouses were strewn around enough to indicate both that Susan wasn't particularly tidy and that she hadn't planned on being gone for any great length of time. And, most telling, the bed was made and a nightgown and robe were laid out on the bed, indicating, as the evidence downstairs did, that Susan had last been here the evening previous to the day her absence was noted.

Charlotte's thoughts went back to that night. She remembered waking to the howling of a dog—most likely Sam. She tried to remember the direction that had come from, and she thought perhaps it was from the direction of Brenda's house, the lot where the murdered woman was found being just beyond that. Charlotte didn't want to read too much into that, though, as she recognized that her mind might just be trying to rationalize events. What was more telling, though, was finding Sam on her doorstep, his leash attached and his paws muddy, on the following morning. If she'd been sharp, she would have collected some of the mud from the crevices in his paws. That might have linked him—and, therefore Susan—to the death scene by Brenda's house. But Charlotte herself had washed away that possible evidence when she had bathed Sam later that day.

As she was thinking these thoughts, Charlotte walked into the second bedroom upstairs—and stumbled onto something that she hadn't, in her remotest conjecturing considered but that now became one more interlocking piece of the puzzle, a flash of light in the darkness.

The room was strewn with items one did not associate with bedrooms. She would only have been curious at the eclectic nature of the furnishings and probably would have written it off to the bedroom being used more as a storeroom than a guest bedroom—if her eyes hadn't gone immediately to the Japanese porcelain tea set that sat in the middle of one of the twin beds—her Japanese porcelain tea set, the one that was missing from the buffet under her dining room window.

The first thought that entered Charlotte's mind was, I've got to get Grady Tarbell to the antique shop in Easton to confirm that the stamp album I found there is his.

What she did next, was to scoop an item up from the other twin bed and march back up River Street to the Vales' B&B.

This time it was Joyce who answered the door, and as soon as she saw what Charlotte was carrying, she broke down into tears. Todd appeared and took Joyce by the shoulders and guided her back into the house. He turned his head to Charlotte and wearily said, "You'd better come in, I suppose."

"So, this *is* your set of silver? You confirm that?" Charlotte asked, when Joyce had stopped blubbering and was sunk into the commodious overstuffed chair Charlotte had occupied on her previous visit. Charlotte was perched on the edge of a hard Windsor side chair, trying not to make it bear all of her weight.

"Yes, it's ours," Joyce answered in a small voice.

"And you realize that I found it in the Wells' house, along with other property that was probably stolen from houses in the village—including something of mine that I know was taken?"

"Yes."

"Did you give this silver to Susan?"

"No."

"And so we understand what the implications of that are, don't we?"

"Yes, I suppose so."

"Does this have anything to do with your secretiveness on Susan being your daughter? And is this why there was the estrangement between you two that I have sensed?" Actually Todd had told Charlotte about the estrangement, but Charlotte was too polite to tattle on him. Todd seemed to realize that and gave Charlotte an appreciative, if startled, look.

"Susan was . . . difficult . . . from childhood. And she was frequently in trouble. I had hoped when she came back here . . . but . . ."

Joyce just let her voice trail off, and, as she rose to leave, Charlotte tried to give her what little hope she could. "This doesn't reflect well on Susan, of course, but it does give us some added hope that she is alive. That is something you can hang on to; I know this is trying for you."

Todd looked up. "Oh, how does this give us hope?"

"It gives us some rationale we didn't have before on why Susan would leave virtually in the middle of the night on her own volition—and thus that she might not be in quite the harm's way we supposed."

And then, when neither of the Vales said anything, while they were digesting and gaining strength from this hope, Charlotte continued. "Did Susan talk to either of you that night—the evening before she was found to have gone missing? Did she mention anything about seeing an unfamiliar woman in a car on River Street that day?"

"No, we didn't talk to her," Todd said. Joyce shook her head in agreement. Todd went on, "But what would that have to do with anything?"

"I saw such a woman that day."

"And you think that maybe she was there watching for Susan—that something Susan had done had brought the woman to town and caused Susan to flee?" Todd asked.

"It's possible. We have so little to go on that every possibility has to be examined."

"And do you know who this woman is? Do you think that she could lead us to Susan."

"No, I don't know who she is. But, yes, there might be a link." But then Charlotte shut up. There indeed was a possibility that there might be a link, but to say anything further about it to the Vales would surely dash any hope that Charlotte had given to them. There was a good chance that, given time to think, the Vales would make the connection themselves. But Charlotte didn't want to tell them that there might be a connection between Susan and the woman found dead on the wooded lot across River Street from their B&B.

Exiting the B&B and turning to walk back to her house, Charlotte's eyes first went to the police car parked in front of the arts center and then to the figures of Jane Cranford and Deputy David

Burch that were standing on the walk beside the cruiser. As she approached, David hailed her, but it was Jane who informed her in a tense, breathy voice, "They've been taken, Charlotte. Sometime last night, someone entered the arts center by one of the back doors and took several of the paintings on loan from the Barnes."

"Last night?" Charlotte asked. "Forced entry?" She addressed this last to David, who opened his mouth to respond, but Jane was still gushing forth in her excitement.

"No. The door looks like it may have been jimmied, Deputy Burch said, but the markings don't match. He thinks it was someone who had a key but who wanted to make it appear like a burglary. And the funniest thing—whoever it was knew where to find the casings for the paintings and knew exactly which ones went with the paintings they took. Do you know what that—?"

"Well, for one thing," Charlotte interjected, as both Jane and David gave her their rapt attention, "I think it means that Susan Purcell is still alive."

Chapter Eight

"Yes, that's mine," Grady said when the stamp album from the Goldsborough Street antique store in Easton was shown to him. Gathered around him, in addition to the distressed store owner, who was twittering and flittering around like a wounded bird caught in a trap—which, in fact, he probably was—were Deputy Burch, Charlotte, and Brenda, the latter of whom had begged to tag along so that she and Charlotte could lunch and boutique crawl in Easton again.

Leaving Grady and Brenda to smooth over the situation with the store proprietor, Charlotte and David Burch moved on to King's Antiques, which Charlotte had seen now displayed an "open" sign in the window.

"After this, I need to talk to you—alone," David said. "That's why I asked Ms. Boynton to stay with Grady."

They entered the store to be met halfway in by a rotund, red-faced little man, all smiles and welcome—at least until he saw the badge David flashed at him. Then it was like seeing water going down a drain as his face closed down into a wash of wariness. Both David and

Charlotte had seen this happen hundreds of times before, and there was no doubt in the minds of either that they were face to face with a fence in stolen goods.

"Yes, yes, I sold that stamp album to Mitch," Stan King acknowledged. "It's more in line with his stock then mine. Of course I had no idea it was stolen."

"Yes, I'd be happy to help identify who I bought it from. She's a recognized local art broker. Yes, yes, that's her," he said as Charlotte showed him the photograph Joyce had given her. "Cynthia Black. No, no, of course I didn't know she really was someone named Susan Purcell. She had a card, yes. But, no, I don't think I kept it."

"Oh those?" he asked nervously as, after she had noticed the wooden art cases propped up beside the back edge of the counter, King was asked where they had come from—and when. "Yes, I did receive those on consignment from Cynthia—from this Purcell woman."

"Recently?"

"When? Why, just this morning."

While David and Stan King watched, with David carefully stationing himself where he could move quickly if King made a run for it either out of the front of the shop or into the back rooms, Charlotte opened a case that was familiar to her—one that she had handled before.

"Do you recognize a genuine Vormeer when you see one, Mr. King?" she asked as she carefully slid the precious landscape oil from the safety of its case. "I'm sure you do—and I don't doubt you know that this one belongs to the Barnes Museum in Philadelphia."

There was little that King could say, and they stood there in a glum little triangle while David Burch called in the town police and they waited for them to arrive.

After King was in custody, David took Charlotte off to the side.

"I'm not surprised the Purcell woman has been unloading stolen goods here. The Easton police have seen the car you described as the one the dead woman was in when you saw her on the street in Hopewell. It's been spotted twice, but they haven't managed to stop it yet. Both times they said a young woman was driving."

"I'd bet it was Susan Purcell," Charlotte said.

"I wouldn't take that bet. But if she's here—and it appears she is, at least as late as this morning—we'll nab her eventually. If she's driving around in the car, she must not know that we have identified it. But there is something we've identified."

"What?"

"The victim. Her name was Pamela Smith, and she's a fraud investigator for the GML Insurance Company. Worked out of New York. They are big on art and life insurance."

Bells rang in Charlotte's brain, but she didn't quite know why—except for the obvious, which David went straight to.

"So, it isn't looking too good for Susan Purcell, is it?"

"No, a lot of things are coming together," Charlotte answered. She didn't know why, but she didn't seem fully satisfied. But that didn't matter. Charlotte hadn't gotten to where she had in the FBI for not being thorough. This case seemed to be coming together, but there were still some *i*'s to dot and *t*'s to cross.

72

"And we're talking murder here," David said. "The medical examiner said she was dead before she went into the water. Blunt object trauma he said. Our teams did a thorough search of the area, so whatever was used to kill her was probably brought in by the killer and taken out again."

"Here are the keys to the Wells house, where Susan was living," Charlotte said. "I guess that's an investigation scene now, and you'd better get a team over there to do a closer search for evidence than I was able to do this morning."

"Will do."

"Oh, and David . . . ask them to be careful of the Japanese porcelain tea set on the guest bed, would you? That's mine."

* * * *

"I felt I needed to talk to you, but I didn't know how to begin. That's why I wanted to come with you to Easton today."

Charlotte and Brenda had started off sitting in the front window alcove of the tea shop on South Washington Street in the shadow of the looming Tidewater Inn across the street, but they had moved back into the interior when it became obvious that those walking down the bricked sidewalk recognized Brenda. The movie tabloids had already located her, at least generally, on the Eastern Shore, so the local residents were on the lookout for the famous actress.

"Yes I gathered as much," Charlotte answered, "Both that you wanted to talk and that, at the same time, it was troubling to you to talk. You were reticent the whole drive from Hopewell. I didn't for a minute think your mind was on what you were saying. Listen, Brenda, you—"

"I feel I need to tell you about my mother's—"

They were talking on top of each other, and both stopped, both with a nervous laugh, in midsentence.

"If you want to tell me anything, that would be fine," Charlotte said. "But you don't have to, you know."

"But you'd advise that I not leave town. Isn't that right?" Brenda said. She was showing a half smile, and Charlotte realized that she melted to that just as much as she did to Brenda's full smile.

"Yes, I guess that's right. It wouldn't look too good if—"

"Don't worry, I'll stay put," Brenda said. "But I want you to know . . . I want you to believe that I had nothing—"

"I don't believe you did, Brenda. Rest assured. I don't believe that of you. And that's not just my emotions speaking—it's my instincts. And my instincts supported me well for over thirty years, so—"

"Thank you. Thank you for that," Brenda said. And the way she said it told Charlotte how heartfelt that was. "That means a lot to me. More than I can say. But I do want to tell you about it."

Charlotte and Brenda broke off and nervously dabbed at their napkins as they were served by a young woman whose eyes were big and glued to Brenda.

Another fan, Charlotte thought. Then, without hesitation, she added in her thoughts: other than me. And it was then that she was sure, that she knew that she wanted Brenda for more than just a casual friend.

"There was some suspicion of me at the time," Brenda was beginning. "But then there was enough suspicion to go around. My father bundled me right off to California—to college and then acting school. He'd seen the potential in my acting career from the beginning. My mother never had. In fact, she wasn't supportive of much of anything that either my father or I wanted to do. And Hopewell was a small town, even then. Everyone knew everyone else's business. And my father moved to New York at the same time. That's when the house was closed up—always maintained well, but closed to the world. Just as both I and my father became. Closed to the world and even, then, to each other. More than my mother died that summer after my senior year."

"You don't have to—" Charlotte said.

"I want to. I've begun now, and I want to finish. And I don't want to sugarcoat it. I became as hateful to my mother in that last year as she'd always been to me—and to anyone else whose path she crossed. I wondered at the time why my father married her. He came from a wealthy family and she had been a waitress from a broken home. I only learned later that he married her because I was coming along—and I don't even think he every really believed that I was his. But that's more to his credit, because he always was loving and kind to me—and attentive, at least up until the moment that glimmer of suspicion was attached to me."

"But surely just not getting along . . . surely that wasn't enough to—"

"Oh, there was more. And everyone in the village knew about it."

The young woman showed up to ask the two if they wanted a refill of their tea or more cookies or more anything at all—and were they finding everything to Their liking? Brenda raised her head and gave the woman a brilliant smile and a thank you, and the young woman floated away on cloud nine.

Charlotte wondered, though, if the waitress had seen the tears in Brenda's eyes that she had seen. Probably not, Charlotte thought. They probably hadn't been visible through the stars in her own eyes. From what little the waitress had said to Brenda and Charlotte, it was obvious that she aspired to be an actress too and now had a dream to carry her through many an audition.

"Go on," Charlotte said, realizing now that the story was too far along for Brenda not to complete it.

"I palled around with a pretty wild bunch at the time," Brenda said. "The village is dominated by retirees now, but then there were several young people, mostly my age, living up and down River Street. And, like any small clique of young people, we thought we owned the world and were reckless in exercising that ownership."

"Joyce and Grady?" Charlotte asked.

"Yes. Joyce was the only one—at least that I knew of—who was caught by it. But there was a group of us girls, including Joyce and me, who were inseparable—and trading off on the few boys who were around . . . and, and on each other."

"Yes?" Charlotte interjected. "But what does that—?"

"What does that have to do with my mother being murdered at the same spot as that young woman's body was found the other day?" It apparently was a rhetorical question, because Brenda drove on. "That was our favorite spot. Our club meeting place. Where we went to smoke our cigarettes and drink our beer and, eventually, to become

76

intimate with each other. And my mother found out about it, and she descended on us like a bat out of hell one evening—she rousted us all out and proceeded to troupe around town and report what she found to the parents of anyone she could identify there. Of course the parents were embarrassed and not all that thankful. But the teens she'd caught—they all hated her for it. And not one of them hated her more than I did. And then she was killed, three nights later. In the same spot."

"So there were suspects enough to go around," Charlotte said.

"Yes, but a few of us—including me—couldn't produce good alibis, and, of course, the greatest suspicion fell on me as the one who was the most abused and had the most to gain by her death. And my sudden departure for the West Coast after that probably didn't help. Regardless, they never did arrest anyone for the death. It wasn't as if anyone in the town missed my mother—and it wasn't long after that before they all had something else to gossip about."

"Oh?"

"Yes, tongues were wagging a different tune when Joyce almost proudly announced that she was pregnant by Grady, who wasn't one of us. He was a new teacher at the school."

"Proudly?" Charlotte prompted.

"Yes, most of the girls wanted him. And, apparently, some of the girls got him. Not just Joyce. Rachel and Jane were after him too."

Charlotte sat up straight in her chair. "Rachel and Jane. Our Rachel and Jane? Rachel Sharp and Jane Cranford? They lived here then?"

"Yes the same. They both lived here then—went to school with me, as Joyce did. Jane's been here forever—or at least I think she went to New York but didn't stay long—but Rachel left the same time I did and, I believe, has only come back on and off. She went to Michigan I think. I'm not surprised she became a doctor. She was always the smart, determined one of us. But she was head over heels for Grady too. She and Joyce fought tooth and nail over him. And then when Joyce got him, the game was over for her. He, of course, had to leave town. He went up to Washington College in Chestertown and stayed on and taught there after he graduated. I was surprised to find he'd moved back here at some point. I rather think he sees that period now as the high point of his life—when there were those who paid attention to him and wanted him."

Charlotte was trying to listen to Brenda, but her mind was racing on having discovered more of the current residents who grew up here.

"Edith Smith," she blurted out. "The woman who lives on the Clagett farm at the edge of the village. Was she here then too?"

Brenda contemplated the question, but after a moment she shook her head and said, "The name doesn't ring a bell. I knew the Clagetts, of course, and there may have been one of them named Edith. But there were so many of them. And young girls? No, I think most of the Clagett children were boys—and they were considered bumptious. They weren't ones who ran with our crowd. Although, wait. I think Kevin might have been a Clagett. He was one of the boys in our group. But I'm rambling now. Is this important?"

"I don't know. It's more a tick at the back of my brain that won't let me alone," Charlotte said. "But it's a revelation to me—like a slow-moving train—to find who was here at that time. Any other townspeople here now who were here then?"

"There's Bonny Levitt, of course. She seemed old then too, but she's in a wheelchair now. And Jason Williams, of course, out at the garage. But others my age? No, I don't think so."

"Well, if you'll indulge me, could you write out a list of anyone you knew here from before?"

"Yes, yes, of course."

"And, needless to say, sooner than later, if you will."

"Yes, yes. I'm happy to do anything you might think will be helpful. But . . ." and here she paused long enough for Charlotte to give her her undivided attention, " . . . but I'm surprised you didn't ask me why I didn't have an alibi to give for the evening my mother died."

"You don't have to—" Charlotte felt this was important—that she was at the moment of truth with Brenda. And it was suddenly important to her that she not blow this. She could either be an investigator or she could go completely on trust.

"I didn't have an alibi I wanted to give, because I was with someone that night . . . one of the girls. And it just wasn't something . . ."

Charlotte let it end there. It might have made a difference if she had asked. But then again it might not have. And at that moment she believed that if she had made Brenda reveal who she'd been with, whatever was blossoming between her and Brenda would die in the bud.

* * * *

It seemed like it was déjà vu all over again when Brenda drove her sports car down River Street as she and Charlotte returned from Easton that afternoon, to find the whole town was out on the street again in front of Brenda's house.

But this time they were turned toward the Vales' B&B. Charlotte took one look at the tableau on the ground between the B&B and the side of Rachel's house and rang 911 on her cell phone with a "damn, I should have foreseen this" comment.

"Can you leave me here and go on to my house and let Sam off the screened porch? He's long overdue for a walk and it looks like I need to be here," Charlotte asked Brenda. "Oh, and there's a camera on the table by one of the chairs on the screened porch. Can you bring that back and get good facial shots of as many of the people here as possible—especially that woman standing apart over there." The request could quite understandably be the occasion for follow-up questions, but Brenda didn't hesitate to fall into the plan and was off again as soon as Charlotte had hauled her bulk out of the low-lying seat of the convertible.

Charlotte was heartened by the groans she heard emanating from Todd's lips as she reach the base of the house, stepping over a ladder on the ground to get to him. He was alive, and it didn't look like the damage was permanent, although one could never tell just from looking at the victim of a fall that there was nothing nasty going on inside.

"What happened?"

"He was all the way up the roof, cleaning out the gutters, apparently," Rachel answered. "I heard the cry and came right out." She was already kneeling beside Todd, feeling for broken bones, and ministering to him.

Charlotte looked around her as she knelt. They were all here— including Edith Smith, who, Charlotte thought, must have her antenna up for any sign of trouble or tragedy.

"Could a couple of you guys go for a stretcher?" Rachel was saying. "You'll find one in my garage. Let's get him into my clinic."

"I don't think that's a good idea, Rachel," Charlotte said. "I think he shouldn't be moved."

"It will be fine. I need to get him to where—"

"I called the rescue squad," Charlotte said. "I really think we need to wait for them. I hear the sirens now."

Rachel looked perturbed, but she didn't argue further. She did open her mouth to say something, but then the attention of all of them were arrested by the other, blaring, unexpected sound, ringing out over the approach siren of the rescue squad vehicle.

Brenda had walked Sam back up the street, wanting to know what was happening. As they approached, Sam tugged on the leash and waded into the congregated group of townspeople fanned out around the figure of Todd on the ground. Joyce was cradling his head in his lap and Charlotte and Rachel were hunched over him while a trembling and crying Jane leaned over Joyce's head. Grady and another man were half way to the garage where Rachel had sent them for a stretcher. Amid all this activity Sam settled down on his haunches and began a god-awful howling to the sky.

The sound sent chills up Charlotte's spine and flipped her thoughts back to just a couple of days previously, when the same howl woke her in the darkest hour of the night.

Chapter Nine

Charlotte was sitting at the Sheraton table, polished to the highest of sheen, and letting her eyes follow the patterns on the chinoiserie wallpaper and in the massive oriental carpet underfoot, savoring a cup of perfect coffee, and listening to the contented soft snore of the husky covering the fronts of her bare feet with his forepaws when the ringing started. It was a hollow, faraway sound, but she recognized that the ring tone was hers, and her brain started skipping ahead, halfway knowing that it wasn't a social call—and probably not good news.

"Your purse is ringing," Brenda said as she entered her dining room, holding the leather pouch emitting the offending sound out at arm's length.

Charlotte smiled up at her, finding Brenda even more beautiful in a robe and slippers than ever before.

"Thanks. The coffee's super," she said, as she reached for the purse.

"Wait until you taste my pecan waffles," Brenda countered with as she handed the purse over and then moved through the swinging door into the kitchen.

Charlotte struggled with digging the cell phone out of her purse, but whoever was calling was both patient and persistent, so it was Charlotte's index finger that deadened the tone.

"Is that you, Ms. Diamond?" the male voice boomed off the signal towers. "I've tried calling your home, but you didn't pick up."

"Yes, it's me, David," she answered the Talbot County deputy sheriff. "It's much too nice a day to be indoors."

Brenda poked her head back into the dining room from the kitchen and gave Charlotte a wink. The two women smiled at the little deception that was not exactly a lie—it indeed looked like it would be a wonderful day to be outside.

"What has or is transpiring?" Charlotte asked. She figured that David must have something important to report if he was calling her at eight in the morning.

"Good news and bad news," he answered. "We've found Susan Purcell. The bad news is that she's dead."

"Oh, Lord," Charlotte answered. "Particulars?"

"Last evening we triangulated reports on sightings of Pamela Smith's blue sedan and found a neighborhood where several residents said they saw such a car parked on the street several days running. It's an area with short-term boarding houses at the edge of Easton. A door-to-door homed us in on where she's been staying. But when we got there, we found her dead. Bludgeoned."

"Oh, dear. I half expected that she was hiding from the murderer rather than being the murderer—and that it was a race to find her. I'm getting rusty, I'm afraid. I've moved too slowly."

"Well, you are miles ahead of me. How do you figure that she was on the lam from the murderer—and why?"

"Logic," Charlotte answered. "Sam, the Wells' husky, pointed to the answer."

"Oh, how so?"

"It was his leash. The only logical reason for him to have been on a leash was that Susan was walking him the night of the murder. I must have gotten through to her on letting him run free. And if she was walking the dog and her house looked like she wasn't planning on abandoning it anytime soon, and then she was missing and driving the victim's car, it didn't seem that she went out to murder someone. On the basis of the combined information, I had to look at other probabilities. Pamela Smith outweighed Susan, significantly, and I don't see Susan as able to swing something heavy enough to do the damage I saw to the victim's skull. Also, Susan was a bad girl, but her MO was theft, not murder. And she didn't go far away; she came back the next night and stole the paintings. It just didn't add up that she was responsible for the dead body. I think it more likely that she saw the killing, let loose of Sam in her surprise and shock, and then left the scene as quickly and conveniently as she could—in Pamela Smith's car."

"That's it? That makes you sure she's not the murderess."

"Well, I'd never say I was positive about anything that didn't have a believable confession backing it up. But there is one other little thing."

"What's that?"

"I called GML Headquarters—the insurance company Pamela Smith works at."

"We've been trying to get a response out of them since yesterday," David said, not without discernible consternation. "How did you—?"

"I had contacts there from my FBI days—close to the top. They were quite cooperative. Pamela Smith was, indeed, on assignment. But she wasn't working an art fraud case—which is what would most likely apply if Susan was her target. She was working life insurance fraud. Susan's parents are both alive and there is no record she ever was married. No one, really, to insure but herself. I think we're looking for an entirely different motive here. They mentioned something about a black widow operation. I've asked them to send a copy of the file to you at the sheriff's office, and they should have faxed it there by now."

"Oh," David responded. "Then this is more complicated than I thought."

"And there's something worse than that, David."

"What?"

"So far this murderer has kept a step ahead of us. How did the murderer get to Susan before we did? That's one of the greatest questions—and most interesting, to me, at least—to this."

"Well," David said after a short pause, "I might have a theory on that. I'll check it out and let you know if there's anything in it—I

86

would be in pretty hot water if I mentioned it and it turned out that there was nothing in it. But for now, if you have a pen and paper, I'll give you the address in Easton. We won't move the body or mess around with anything else until you get here. I won't be here, though. I'm off to the sheriff's office to check a few things."

"I'm on the way," Charlotte said after noting the address down. And as she clicked off on the call, she was already standing and calling out to Brenda in the kitchen.

"Hold the waffles, Brenda, and get dressed, please. We're off to Easton and then to Annapolis."

A head appeared from around the edge of the swinging door. "We? You're taking me with you?"

"I sure am," Charlotte said, trying to pull up her most winning and confident smile to flash at Brenda. "I don't want to let you out of my sight now."

"Ooo. Possessive. I'll have to think whether I like that," Brenda answered, but she smiled broadly and dipped back into the kitchen, and Charlotte heard the sounds of ingredients and pans being swiftly put away.

As soon as Brenda was out of sight, the smile on Charlotte's face turned to a worried frown. Not wanting Brenda out of her sight didn't mean quite what Brenda thought it meant. Increasingly, Charlotte's well-tuned brain was telling her that it wasn't a coincidence that Pamela Smith and Brenda's mother were murdered in the same, remote spot. Chances were good that Brenda herself was in danger— and the only way Charlotte could be sure Brenda was safe was to keep her close by.

* * * *

Charlotte introduced Brenda to a former assistant of hers in the lobby of the FBI office in Annapolis. Margaret Fancel was immediately star struck and, even after being told why, was only too delighted to walk Brenda down to the shops at the Annapolis harbor while Charlotte took her digital camera up to her old offices to do some quick face recognition work and to conduct a search through the files. Brenda was happy for the company, although she declared that she could have found the harbor herself.

Charlotte wasn't really sending Margaret along for the company. As star struck as the young FBI agent was, she was also quick to assess and react to situations and was a crack shot with the gun she kept in the holster under her jacket. Having just discovered the wonders of Brenda, Charlotte was taking no chances with her well-being.

Charlotte had left her cell phone in the glove compartment of Brenda's car, not wanting to set off the collection of security-check machines in the FBI office between the entrance and the labs on the third floor. She was to think in days to come that this had been a mistake.

Two hours later the two were speeding back to Hopewell in Brenda's sports car, with Charlotte frantically trying to raise Deputy David Burch on her cell phone.

At length, the sheriff's office called her—but the call wasn't from him—it was about him.

"Sorry, Ma'am, his cruiser was sideswiped off the road on route 50 between Easton and Hopewell. He said he was on his way there to make an arrest. And he said he was trying to get hold of you, but you weren't picking up."

"Is he—?"

"No, he'll pull through. But he's still unconscious. The cruiser turned right over. I'm told the driver's side is a mess."

"Blue paint on the swipe marks?" Charlotte asked.

"Yes, how did you know?"

Charlotte didn't answer. She had information to convey and time was of the essence. "Does your office know who he was going to arrest?"

"No, Ma'am. He said it was sort of a delicate matter. He'd been to a judge, but he wouldn't tell us who he was going after."

"Is Sheriff Wainwright there?"

"No, Ma'am, he's not. Would you like us to—?"

"Good. No don't track him down. I know who David was going to arrest. And I know the car you're looking for. I'm going to give you the information, and you are to put some patrol cars out on the road and get them to Hopewell as soon as possible. Oh, and call the county hospital and have someone stationed at Todd Vale's bedside— and David's too—and get a couple of police officers over there and on their hospital doors."

"Yes, Ma'am. As soon as you hang up."

"And, officer . . . don't track the sheriff down or tell him what's in motion as long as you can keep from doing so."

As she clicked off, Charlotte turned to Brenda and said, "Can this buggy go any faster?"

Brenda smiled, hunkered down in her seat, and muttered a "You betcha" as her foot depressed on the gas pedal.

Chapter Ten

"When did you figure out that it was Rachel Sharp?" Brenda asked, as she handed Charlotte a margarita and settled down in the Adirondack chair next to Charlotte's facing the lake and set where the dock at her house met the river's edge.

Charlotte sat there for a moment in silence, holding her drink in one hand and scratching Sam's crown with the other as he sat beside her and panted happily. Her eyes went to the other side of the river, where the bottom of an orange sun had just touched the top of the shadowed tree line. The undersides of cumulus clouds scudding in layers across the sky reflected the sun's waning rays and promised a spectacular sunset show to come.

"I'll admit that I didn't even consider her until you told me she had been raised here and was part of your crowd when you mother was killed. I try to keep an open mind, but from the moment I found out that Pamela Smith's was the second murder in that exact spot, I paid more attention to those who were here when your mother died than to those who weren't. I don't believe in coincidences all that much. I know they do happen, but I don't run on the assumption that they have."

"And for a while I was a key suspect, wasn't I?"

"For a while, yes. I didn't want you to be, of course. But my training wouldn't permit me to discount the possibility. I—"

"That's quite all right. I wouldn't have wanted you to be any less professional and thorough than you were. It freed me . . . at last. My mother's death has weighed on me all of these years. I never thought it was Rachel. I always was more inclined toward Jane or Joyce—or Grady, even, although I guess I always did think of him as too wimpy to carry through with anything that violent."

"As was I for a while."

"And in a way, I *was* responsible for my mother's death. Rachel did it for me. She saw how miserable I was and she did it for me. And having gotten the taste of it, she just went on doing it."

"You can't blame yourself. You didn't ask her to do it. Rachel was responsible for her own actions—even then, as a much younger woman."

"Ah, those triangular affairs. We were so young, so willing and ready. Invincible and wanting to try it all. And so cliquish. I pursued Jane, while Jane pursued Rachel, and Rachel pursued me. And, at the same time Rachel and Jane pursued that divine young teacher, Grady. Not me, of course. Then . . . even then I was set on a different course. And Grady was willing to please them all, while . . . interestingly enough, pursuing me. I laugh now when I see Grady, see the doddering old man he has become. But it was cruel of Joyce . . . to deny him like that."

92

"I wonder if all small villages are like this," Charlotte mused.

"I rather think they are," Brenda answered. "And it's rather comforting in its own way. Hopewell has grown old with the rest of us. There probably are no seething undercurrents here anymore."

"I wonder. I rather imagine there are—but just with a whole different cast of characters."

"I suppose you may be right. But I asked you about when you knew it was Rachel, and then we went off on a tangent. A pleasant tangent, of course. I love tangenting with you. But the case, Rachel."

"Ah, yes. It was Todd and Sam that jolted it in place for me—although until I went to the FBI lab in Annapolis, I wasn't sure. And I do think it important to be sure. But I sometimes wonder about that. If I had operated on instinct—if we'd sped back to Hopewell as soon as David told me that Pamela Smith was working on a case for GML, I might have made it back to Hopewell before Todd was pushed off that ladder."

"Pushed? And what does Todd have to do with it? He wasn't one of our original teenage set here—or perhaps he was and I just haven't recognized him. Kevin Clagett in disguise perhaps?"

"Todd was head of the fraud investigations at GML before he retired. That was a coincidence really—and one that I should have paid more attention to. He was completely apart from the issue, really, but Rachel had been on the lam so long for so many years and watching her back so carefully that it didn't look like a coincidence to her."

"But, what—?"

"Rachel thought that Todd was on to her—somehow recognized her from a case open from the time he was with GML. She had married that series of men under assumed names and used her medical knowledge to murder them without suspicion until she had done it so often that the people at GML began to put her face to different, similar large payouts. When she learned that an investigator had come into the area from GML, which was one of the companies she had taken hard in her black widow scheme, she assumed that Todd had blown the whistle on her, and she tried to kill him by pushing him off the ladder while he was cleaning his gutters."

"But she was there; she was giving him medical attention."

"Yes, she was the first one there—the very first one. She practically admitted it at the time, and I wasn't listening. And did you notice how irritated she was that I had called the rescue squad? She wanted to get him into her clinic where she could finish the job. That alone raised signals at the time—and then there was Sam, which brought it together for me. I just didn't know why yet, and I wanted to know why. I was being a bit self-indulgent."

"Sam? You did mention Sam, didn't you?"

"Yes, Sam's our real sleuth here," Charlotte said. And, hearing his name spoken, Sam raised up on his haunches and put his muzzle in Charlotte's lap. She took a moment to pet him down and rub her nose on his hairy cheek, which he thoroughly enjoyed. "Not just our sleuth; he was our key witness all along, and we weren't appreciating that well enough."

"Key witness?"

"Yes. His howling in the night timed the murder. And then, when you brought him to the B&B when everyone was gathered around Todd on the ground, perhaps no one else noticed, but when he set off on his howling there, he was face to face with Rachel. And the look on Rachel's face was as precious as it was damning. Sam was there, in the woods by your house, when Pamela Smith was murdered, murdered because Rachel had learned Smith was closing in on her. And Susan Purcell was there, too. That's why she ran. She saw Rachel at the murder scene—and she panicked and let loose of Sam's leash and stumbled back out to the road and took the first escape route she saw. She took Pamela Smith's blue sedan and drove all of the way to Easton. She didn't leave altogether right away, though, as she was still in the middle of what she was here for."

"Which was to steal us blind, right?"

"Right. She was pilfering from local houses—taking advantage of her knowledge from her early life of who here had what and of our quaint local custom of not locking our doors. My Japanese porcelain tea set had the misfortune of being put in my dining room window where she could easily see it. And with Susan's art training, she knew what was worth going for. Of course she was here primarily to steal those paintings from the Barnes. Her whole effort to get the arts center gallery established was focused on that scheme."

"An altogether unpleasant young woman—but I'm sorry to say that I can see Joyce in her."

"Yes, I feel a responsibility for what happened to her. I led Rachel to her, and my rustiness off the mark at least contributed to her death. Of course, Rachel had been looking for her from the moment she'd stumbled on Rachel doing away with Pamela Smith."

"How can you say you contributed to Susan's death? And this is the second time you've indicated that Rachel had knowledge of the investigation. What—?"

"The sheriff. Sheriff Wainwright. He didn't do it intentionally, of course. But Rachel used him. She had been doing so for some time. It was part of her protection plan and it worked like a charm."

"I don't under—"

"David Burch fell into this first. He's as cautious as I am, but if he had told me what he suspected when he suspected it, he might have saved himself a trip to the hospital. When I suggested that someone was keeping tabs on the investigation and staying one step ahead of us, he immediately thought of Rachel. He knew that the sheriff and Rachel were an item but were keeping it as secret as possible because the sheriff is married.

"Rachel was using him, though—pumping him for information on what we knew and when we knew it. Thus, she knew a GML investigator was on her trail because Smith had to register with the sheriff's office and Rachel had her antenna up for just such a situation. And then she wheedled out of the sheriff our progress in finding Susan. And she got to Susan before we did. David was on his way to arrest her, the files faxed from GML to him having included photographs he identified as Rachel and then assuring him she was the one. Not wanting to get the sheriff involved, he got the arrest order himself from a judge and was on his way to find Rachel, when she found him instead, driving in Pamela Smith's car that Susan had taken."

"All so complicated and yet so simple," Brenda said, with a sigh.

"In the end, I'd say that Rachel probably did herself in. She was possibly being just a bit too clever. If there hadn't been two murders in the same spot, there's little chance we would have backed into solving this by connecting it with your mother's murder. She no doubt lured Pamela Smith into the woods somehow, but why she picked that exact spot seems risky vanity to me. Perhaps knowing you had returned—and thus were yet another danger to her—she wanted to cast suspicion on you. But we probably won't know for some time."

"Do you think they will catch her?"

"Yes, I'm confident they will. She's running out of room and luck. We'll find her, I'm sure. The damaged blue sedan was found in Baltimore. She's on the FBI's scope now. They'll find her."

Brenda turned her eyes to the developing sunset for a few minutes and sighed her contentment.

"And this Edith Smith? A red herring?"

"Yes, I'm afraid so—but yet a confirmation that I haven't let my skills atrophy totally. She does strongly resemble a serial killer in an open case I dealt with for years. And the Edith Smith of the Clagetts' farm is a cousin of the woman we're looking for in that case. Thank God for the new face recognition database the FBI is building. I'm glad I put that bothersome worry to rest. Just a strong resemblance one bears to the other. Still, it points to what a small world we live in."

"Yes, it does," Brenda said.

"And it gives me something to do while I'm wasting away here," Charlotte said, with a laugh. "If I watch Edith Smith closely enough, perhaps her cousin will come to me at last—I certainly spent enough years trying to track her down on her own turf."

97

"I thank God it's such a small world," Brenda said, her voice ground softer. "It made it easier for me to find you. And I certainly hope that we can not just waste away here after having found each other."

Charlotte turned her eyes toward Brenda and saw that there were tears on Brenda's cheek. She felt she was tearing up herself.

And at the moment Sam raised his muzzle and began to howl at the sinking sun, sending it tendrils of orange and yellow and purple and blue rays up into the scudding clouds.

"I think you need to do something about your dog," Brenda said with a rich laugh. "He'll raise the neighborhood. I would have said he'd raise the dead, but I think we've had enough of that on River Street for a while."

"Oh, let him howl," Charlotte responded. "He deserves having the pleasure of that. Let's leave him and go into the house and do some howling of our own."

"I'm game, of course. But I thought we'd planned to get out on the river in the twilight. But then perhaps we have blathered out here too long. The sun has almost left us now."

"I think we need to buy a new, larger sailboat before we go out on the river again," Charlotte responded. "Putting your Laser and my Penguin together, we still only have two one-woman sailboats. It's not only that I fear I really will drown you if we get out on the water at the same time in those two boats, but I also fancy the thought of the two of us in one boat together."

Brenda turned and smiled her radiant smile and said, "Yes, I rather fancy that too."

As she struggled out of the garden chair, Charlotte was struck with two thoughts. Brenda had said Sam was her dog and she hadn't demurred. Until now, she hadn't given it a thought—but at least for the moment Sam *was* her dog—and that made her feel less alone, more content. But not just that. No, not just that by a long shot. Now there was Brenda as well.

♥

Olivia Stowe

Olivia Stowe is a published author under different names and in other dimensions of fiction and nonfiction and lives quietly in a university town with an indulgent spouse and two demanding Siamese cats

www.cyberworldpublishing.com